Vagina

::The Zine

Hillary-Anne Crosby // Editor-In-Chief

With its quarterly publications, Vagina provides a space for women contributors to share their creative work with the public. The zine features a unique variety of opinions, passions, and observations from our contributors.

www.TheVaginaZine.com

Hello friends,

Welcome to *Vagina*'s first full-color issue! This dream has been a long time coming for me and it's all thanks to you! When I founded the zine over three years ago, I could not have imagined that this would happen -- that I'd be reading emails from girls all over the world, that I'd be neck-deep in hundreds of submissions, that a generous online community would raise enough money to make this issue a real dream come true.

But here we are. And I have to say, it does feel like a dream.

The next seventy-odd pages feature some truly incredible pieces, whether they be stories, thoughts, poems, or advice. I started *Vagina* because I wanted a place for women to share their work and here it is. I don't know most of these girls and I don't personally identify with all of the pieces but each of these contributors self-identifies as a woman and each has a voice that deserves to be heard.

Thanks for listening. Thanks for supporting these women. Thanks for supporting *Vagina*.

Sincerely,
Hillary-Anne
Editor-in-Chief

+ + + + + + + + + + + + + + + + + + +

Cover Design: Valerie Wolf
Cover Photograph: Paula Wolf
Custom Lettering: Lindsay Eyth

Table of Contents

Prose

What I Meant When I Said I Meant It // Bee Walsh

Because I've had two fingers pressed into the soft spot at the base of my neck between my collar bones for twenty minutes. Because I'm worried that my arrhythmia is really in my head. Because as soon as I remove my hand from my chest, my heart skips forward and doubles back. Because maybe it's just trying to remind me that I don't have a heart, I am heart.

Because when my heart pauses, it makes me swallow, hard, like my body thinks that's how I breathe, by swallowing in my stomach and not in my lungs. This is what I mean when I say it's hard to find the air. I've been putting it in the wrong place all these years.

Because something about using how I threw up after the first time I listened to Pianos Become The Teeth's "The Lack Long After" as a metaphor against making new friends.

Because we have all entered rooms and wept.

Because I'm translating things from English to English. Because I only see half of what I'm writing. Because I call people until they answer and that says more than anything I could.

Because it's as if I purposefully put myself out there in all the wrong ways in hopes people will be reproachable in their dealings with me. Because on a scale of not getting it to getting it, you get it. Because you read me like book, a reluctant book, a book with a slow beginning.

Because what would I do without you.

Because something about putting my two fingers pressed up into the soft triangle at the base of my neck, where my collar bones constantly miss one another, for what seemed like but was certainly not the better part of a year. Because there's certainly no way that I created something in my head that I felt in my chest. Because maybe I just described the last ten years of my life.

Because in translating this from English to English and back again, something is going to get lost. Because sometimes the curtains only look blue to the author when you or you or I or you would call them Pacific, which is exactly what standing on the shore with the water on the wrong side is like.

Because I have this idea that if I put the air where it goes and stop vomiting in public private places, I'll be less attuned to how much my building shakes on a daily basis. Because, well, what if it's not the building.

What then.

Prose

What I Meant When I Said I Meant It, Pt. II

// Bee Walsh

On mornings like this, I used to dig my first two fingers into the soft spot at the base my neck to feel own heart beating. Somewhere along the line, I wasn't able to get them deep enough to feel it anymore. These days, I spend the first few hours I'm awake jamming my fingers in between my fifth and sixth ribs, practically clawing through my own chest. *Your heart is a muscle, the size of your fist, keep on loving, keep on fighting, hold on your life.**

Mornings like these I make decisions with my fingers between my ribs, like to remove myself from your public letter writing, and to distract myself from instead of admitting to what my own beating heart is telling me. I'm the one saying it's not okay now. Pinch bruises prove a distraction. Traffic light-long day-dream vacations to places I wish I never left, as well. I go everywhere without you. Even the middle-of-the-night change of destination that was your own idea isn't able to take my mind off my own beating heart. But in the morning, I'm left desperate to get inside myself.

Because something about putting my two fingers pressed up into the soft triangle at the base of my neck, where my collar bones constantly miss one another, for what seemed like but was certainly not the better part of a year. Because there's certainly no way that I created something in my head that I felt in my chest. Because maybe I just described the last ten years of my life.

*from Ramshackle Glory's song, "Your Hearst is a Muscle"

3 Things I Know Next To Nothing About

// Kathryn Bailey

My sadness is not a darkness, it is like light that reaches and spreads faster than my eyes can catch it hitting every single thing it can like when I can't sleep and the light from the bathroom stretches down the hallway even hitting the kitchen a little bit and my sadness is not cold, it's hot enough to change every single thing it touches like how they said in chemistry that there is no such thing as cold there is just an absence of warmth, like ice cubes melt rather than freeze the water around them and that's why I can't keep up with the sadness inside me when it melts and changes everything around me. It blinds me like sunlight in January.

The boy I thought I was going to marry tried to explain to me something about physics, about how friction exists because the atoms of the two objects latch together like a zipper and when they move they get pulled apart so that's why tires skid to a halt and that's why it was so hard to pull away from him, our skin resisting the separation because let's not cause friction let's just lie here, bodies at rest. I'm not sure if I completely got the theory right but I ripped our atoms apart anyway.

When we were young we convinced ourselves of that old wives tale that the white marks on our fingernails meant someone was thinking about us and god I always clung to that, looking down at my scarred knuckles and my short pink fingernails and seeing one or two glimpses of hope that I really did cross your mind because you sure as fuck were on mine, your mouth and hands and quiet little moans and your fingernails in my skin but then one day I found out the white marks are calcium deposits and you haven't thought of me in months.

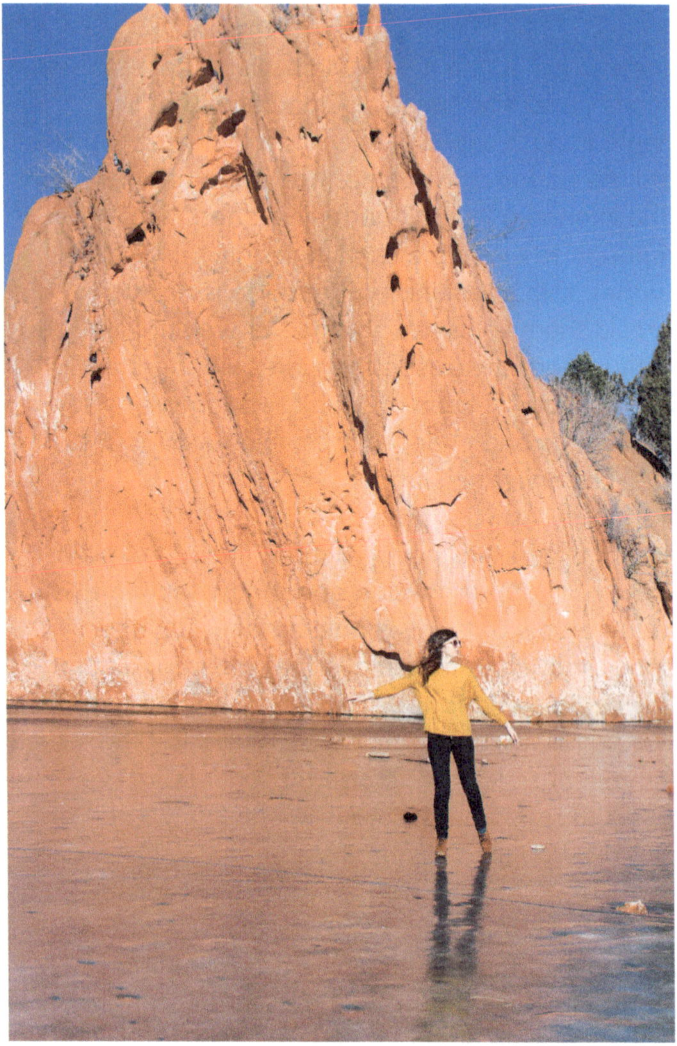

// By Amy Searle

Cheer Up
// Courtney Leigh

On the practice field, our bodies moved together, flawless and taut and fluid. We practiced the same 1-2-3-4 over and over, the same rhythm, the same motion, and it always began on my count. R and F stood across from each other, R to my right and F to my left. K, our flyer, stood between them, and I stood behind K. I placed my hands on K's waist, slid my fingers a little under her shirt, needing the stickiness of her skin on the palm of my hand. She placed her foot on their hands, her hands on their squared shoulders. We locked ourselves so tightly together. We leaned our weight into the mass of interwoven bodies. I felt the stillness between us.

"One, two," I counted, my voice hitching up on the "two." The rest of the counts were silent, but we'd done this so many times our brains effortlessly clicked them out. K dipped down on the three and pushed up on the four, keeping her stomach, her shoulders, her ass, and her thighs tight. My fingers dug into the bone of her hips. It was vicious how I gripped her. But then F, R, and I flcked all of her upward, casual in the way we could throw a girl's body. All we needed was a second and then she was flying away from us, up and up and up until she hit the crest of her momentum.

There at the top her legs spread, hitting a toe-touch of such exquisite release. Everything, so tight and compact and balled up, now suddenly exploding. Her insides out.

Exposed and vulnerable and free. It wasn't in front of anyone. It was practice and it was just for us.

And we fucking had it.

* * *

Late at night, when our parents thought we were asleep, we were sitting on blankets in the grass with boys, and R was across from me. We were so intertwined. K and F were somewhere else nearby. I didn't care about K and F, the shit they did. It was me and R with two boys beside us, between us, all of us sprawled and glancing and tangled a little. The stars in the sky above this small town weren't real. I couldn't believe in them or the big things they tried to tell me. I didn't look at them for long.

R needed to stretch, she said. She was so sore. All of those weights Coach made us lift. All of those squats. Those jumps. Those stunts. Those sit-ups. All of that tumbling. We carried it in our bodies. She could use a massage.

It was dark, but we saw her legs moving away from each other. Her hips rolling forward, and then there she sat, split, in the splits, ankles miles apart, fingers kneading into thigh and calf, digging deeper and deeper into flesh, her body folding over itself and her moaning softly between us.

She knew what she was doing. I mean, I think she knew what she was doing. She had to. The boys were quiet. I was quiet. Our silence raged through me, and I kept it inside. I kept it. I kept my knees tucked up to my chest and glared at her performance through the dark. I had never seen a face look so perfect in moonlight.

* * *

A Captain's List of Everyday Concerns

- Will J get drunk after the game and show up late to Saturday practice again?
- Algebra is not that fucking hard, A. Do your homework. Pass your test. The end.
- I bet nobody remembers the new cheer we practiced on Wednesday.
- K looked surly at lunch. Guy problems most likely. Maybe talk to her later?
- That boy touched me on the bus.
- Thong or bikini cut beneath my hot pants this week?
- Can't forget to shave my legs before the game.
- K better not shave her legs. She better not lotion either. Casually remind K of that flyer from cheer camp who broke her tailbone because she shaved her legs and her backspot couldn't hold on to her.
- Need a theme for next week's pep rally. Talk to R.
- R's thighs look better in the white uniform. Mine look better in the red.
- That boy touched me on the bus.
- I weigh two and a half pounds less than I did last week.
- Spanish worksheet. English essay. Pre-cal lesson. European History definitions.
- C's getting fat. Thank god she's not a flyer.
- Stop thinking about the boy on the bus. You have your license now. Stop thinking about him.
- Coach said more showmanship. Bigger smiles,

girls. Bigger. *Bigger*. More teeth. Show them teeth.
•Is it okay to masturbate again tonight?

* * *

Did you hear about Bianca? About her and Dale? After the game last Friday? In his pickup truck in the school parking lot? They fucked so hard he ripped her. Doggie style. He ripped her apart. Oh my god, remember freshman year? Nancy and that Dr. Pepper bottle up her cooch? She's disgusting. Kristen slept with Justin last night. I don't think Allie wears anything under her hot pants. Her ass is *always* hanging out. I was scared when Jake and I did it the first time. He's huge. Like really huge. I didn't think that thing could go in. Kristen totally had sex with with Mark last night. You thought R was still a virgin? No way. She lost it a long time ago. She never told you that? I thought she was like your best friend or something. She did it with Cal Clifford. Sophomore year maybe? Listen, this shit is scary. You know Jimmy Wright's party in May? Well, apparently Maria got so wasted she blacked out. She woke up at like four in the morning in the back of his Bronco. Her pants were undone and, like, pulled down a little. I heard there was blood or something. Kristen fucked Diego last night. Slut.

I didn't know if things like this were true.

* * *

This was what we waited for—the lights, the grass, the grunting, slamming testosterone, the brassy notes of our alma mater. Our flyaway skirts swishing. Our glistening legs flashing up near our faces. The lines of our shoulders and our stomachs and our hips twisting in the same direction. Our syncopation. Our deep, throaty yells. Our teeth. The flick of our wrists. Our bent knees. Our sturdy ankles. The fervor of us all together. On the track. Bouncing, flinging, thrusting our energy between man-boys and bleacher.

V was our darling. Our tiniest flyer and our best tumbler. She was the only one who could do a full, who could hurl her four feet of perfectly shaped muscle fearlessly backward. She could flip and twist all the way around at the same time. She was magnificent. We loved throwing her in basket tosses, five, six, or even seven feet in the air when our adrenaline pumped like it did now. But sometimes she didn't feel like it. That was the problem with having a darling. Sometimes she ate something weird. Or she had cramps. Or a migraine. Or pain in her back. Sometimes a darling suffered these types of maladies.

Earlier, in the first quarter, I asked her to do more jumps after each cheer. I'd singled out our little darling because she was slacking off and needed someone to tell her. But during halftime she'd eaten some weird-tasting nachos, she said, two minutes into the third quarter. Her stomach hurt. She couldn't possibly do a basket toss now.

Coach: *Showmanship, girls! Smile! Show your teeth! More teeth! Show them your teeth!*

But I saw you do a back tuck five minutes ago, V.

Prose

It just now started hurting.

Do you need to sit down?

Well, I think I can still cheer...but yeah, maybe no basket tosses?

If you can tumble, you can do basket tosses.

It's only a little queasy. I'm sure I can still do the cheers.

If you can't do basket tosses, you can't tumble. You can't do jumps. You can't even move. You might as well go sit down for all you're worth to us right now.

Show me your teeth, girls! Smile! Smile! Smile! Let me see your teeth!

R caught my eye. Did she think I should let it go, leave it at that, allow V to have her moment? She probably did, but that was why I was captain and not R. Why I was the one with "bitch" in my spine, in my strut, in the gums of my teeth. Why I watched my girls with knife eyes, looking and looking and always looking for their soft, plastic, disposable edges to cut off, to whittle away, to excise and destroy. I saw it. I saw how we could be so much better and more and bigger than this.

These girls didn't understand. Not even R understood. She couldn't see beneath our sleek bodies, our too-tight, too-short skirts, the spandex over our asses, our glossy lips and shiny ponytails. She didn't know why we dressed ourselves up like this. She didn't notice the deepest, darkest, most shameful craving inside each and every one of us. She only wanted the glow of the lights and the awesome words to put on her college application. She wanted the boy-glances in the hallway. She didn't notice or understand the animal under the stares, the pawing, the grunting, and the snarling in our honor. The slobbering want that clamored all around our bodies. Everything we did with these bodies – the tossing, the kicking and flailing, the makeup and paint, the thrusts of our hips – it was all saying the same thing. The thing we wanted most.

Look at me. Please look at me.

And that was exactly what we got. It was all we got. It was maybe all some of us would ever get. I was supposed to learn it and wield it and never get caught by it. I was supposed to shimmer out of its way, evade its capture, never ever stop, never ever submit to all the things man-boys wanted from me underneath those looks. But this was for them, wasn't it? At least, that was what I felt crawling, blooming, burning underneath everything. That we all belonged to them. I wasn't to open my mouth. I wasn't to utter a word. Just smile. Show those teeth. Shake those hips and flick that hair and hope to be noticed before K or V or F or even R.

But fuck that.

I didn't want to care about the looks. I already cared too much as it was. I had something better, I told myself, and I wasn't going to give it up, not to anyone or anything. It didn't come out softly or gently. I didn't try to make it sweet. It wasn't pretty. And that didn't matter anyway. What mattered, the only thing that mattered, was that I cared deeply for my stupid, beautiful girls and the things I could make of them. The things we could make of ourselves.

Listen to me, V. Either do the basket toss or go sit down next to coach like the little wimp you are.

Smile.

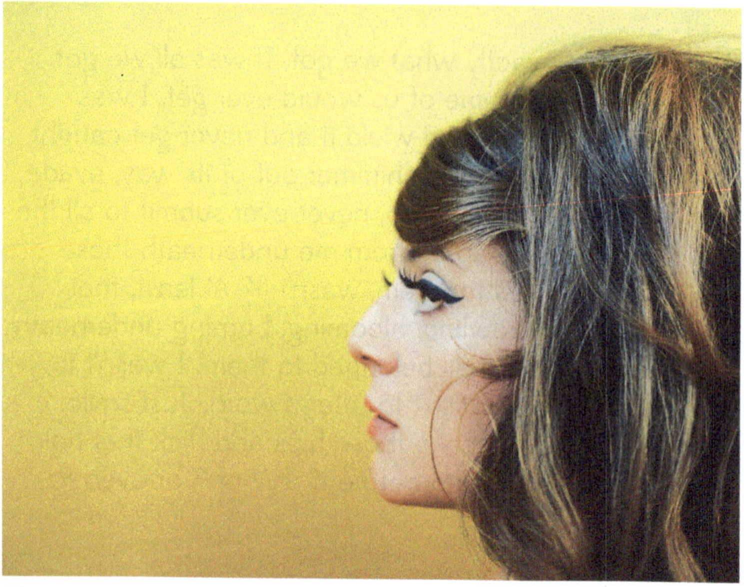

// By Elaine Huang

Victims & Our Voices // Hillary-Anne Crosby

If we're going to get anywhere in terms of people treating people like people, we're going to need to be as critical of those we idolize as we are of those we don't. We're going to have to hold everyone equally accountable for their actions and not just look the other way when that means admitting they're not all that we want them to be.

Despite allegations from too many of our leaders, we're not actually facing an epidemic of people lying about being victims of sexual abuse. We don't have hoards of folks accusing others of rape, pedophilia, or really any abuse just for the heck of it. And I can assure you that it's just the same for our beloved directors, favourite athletes, or talented musicians.

I'm not judge-and-jury, I'm not a psychiatrist, and I'm not Dylan Farrow. But I'm a person and a victim of sexual abuse and I understand the courage it took for Dylan to tell that story and the humanity required of us to not question it.

We have a backlog of over a half-million rape kits, a justice system that isn't always just, and a culture that more often than not is telling a victim to just stay quiet and not upset anyone. Please, don't be a part of these problems. Please, don't assume that a victim is lying. Please, don't assume they're in it for the publicity. Please, don't make it any harder for victims (and perpetrators) to come forward with their stories.

Every time I see a friend or family member defending a rapist, or worse – just saying the words *I Don't Care*, it reaffirms my decision to stay silent on the names of my past abusers and it reminds me that I'm a powerless victim. And I know that's not right but I think to myself, They don't even know that celebrity, they'd never believe me over their friend. I'm not speaking for everyone, I don't know how others feel. But I'm just one voice in a sea of many, many other victims who face this same struggle every time we see you defend an abuser.

You're not the judge-and-jury, you're not the psychiatrist, and you're not the victim. But you're a person with a voice and I hope that you'll use that voice to hold people responsible for their actions, even when those are people you look up to. I know that can require a lot and maybe more than you feel you can give, so I'm only asking you to please, please never use your voice to make the victim feel any more like a victim.

* * *

It really bares noting that I don't personally prefer the term Victim because I feel that Survivor is far more accurate and really conveys the strength we all have to not let our horrible experiences define us. That being said, I wrote this piece because conversations that defend sexual abusers leave me (falsely) feeling as if that strength isn't really there and that is exactly why I chose to use Victim here.

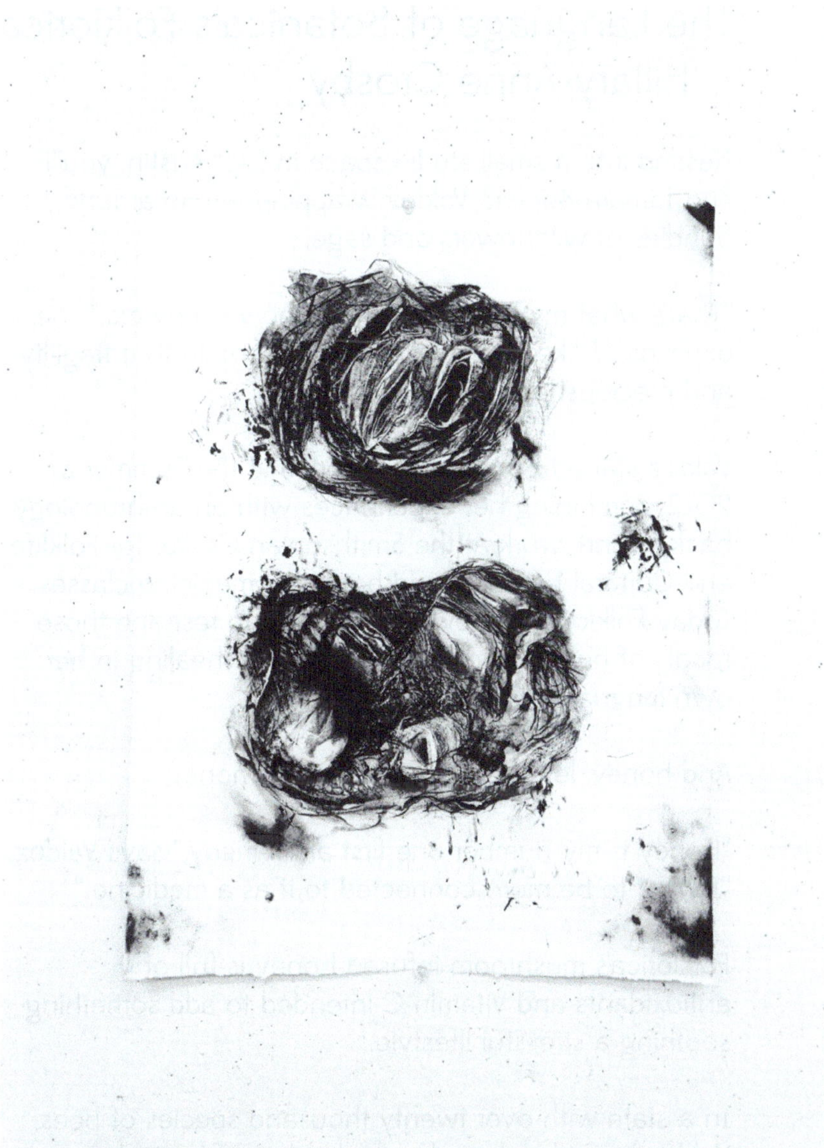

// By Kendal Kulley

Opinion

The Language of Botanicals Folklorica // Hillary-Anne Crosby

Nestled into a small studio space in East Austin, you'll find Tamara Becerra Valdez wrapping thread around bundles of wildflowers and sage.

"That's what my language is right now -- flowers," she explains. "I like making things that contain that fragility and preciousness."

Valdez started Botanicals Folklorica in the Summer of 2012, combining her experiences with an anthropology background, work at the Smithsonian Center for Folklife and Cultural Heritage, and botanical medicine classes. Today Folklorica is how she chooses to reshape those facets of herself and retell traditions of healing in her own language, the flowers.

And honey, let's not forget about the honey.

"Honey is my number one first aid remedy," says Valdez. "I want to be more connected to it as a medicine."

Folklorica's mushroom-infused honey is full of antioxidants and Vitamin C intended to add something soothing a stressful lifestyle.

In a state with over twenty thousand species of bees, Valdez considers herself an advocate of honeybees; she takes care to form relationships with local beekeepers and to ensure that the bees are being cared for naturally.

The pairing of Valdez's precious creations with hardy Texas plants or resilient honeybees is sure to have a lasting effect on the botanical medicine community. To find out more about Botanicals Folklorica, visit www.BotanicalsFolklorica.com or take a look-see at Las Cruxes boutique in Austin, Texas.

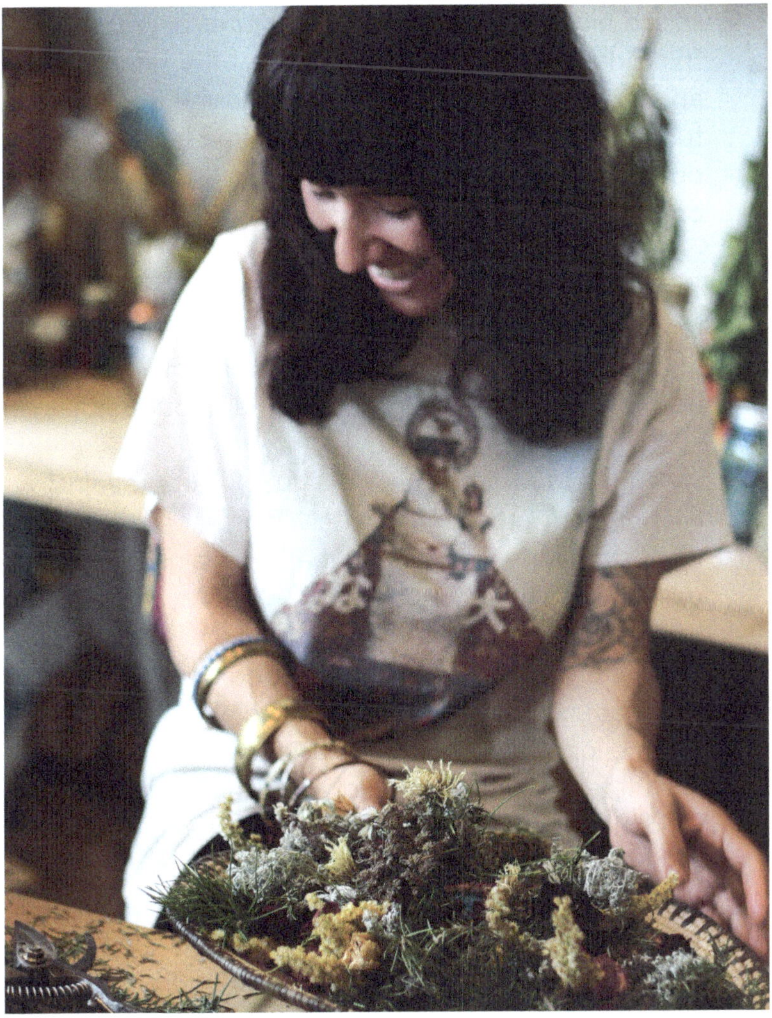

Opinion

The State of the World
// Basia Borodziewicz

From the depths of our armchairs, toes sweating in fuzzy slippers, we sip our morning coffee in solidarity with all those that greet red rising suns, shining on spilled blood still fresh with hope for a fairer future. In solidarity, we lament the losses of the fathers and mothers swept from this earth in the frenzy of furious protests for causes long diluted by dictatorial opportunists. We write a check, in solidarity with the orphans that face a hopeless future born of hope.

In solidarity, we learn enough family history to remember our vociferous ancestors who similarly yelled at an apathetic world – "Help us, World! Help us! Did you not say that it would stop at us, end at our borders?"

When did terror become a platitude? Tanks against foot soldiers, drones against civilians, fanatic ideologies against poverty, mental occupation against identity, sarin gas against starvation.

Did the first people play a game of exclusion, balancing prodigal instincts with guilt-induced empathy? Is one lifetime long enough for disillusionment to take hold or does it take generations, slowly strangling humanity? Solidarity becomes a mawkish farce championed by the soft skinned privileged.

We the people of the United States of Humanity are coming up for a breath of fresh air from the turmoil.

Opinion

What is privilege but a reprieve in which we desperately cling to stability pushing others into the peripheries? We play our game of exclusion to allow for peaceful walks and boisterous gatherings because soon, inevitably, the tables will turn, and we will be staring into the face of indifference like two mirrors perpetuating an endless cycle.

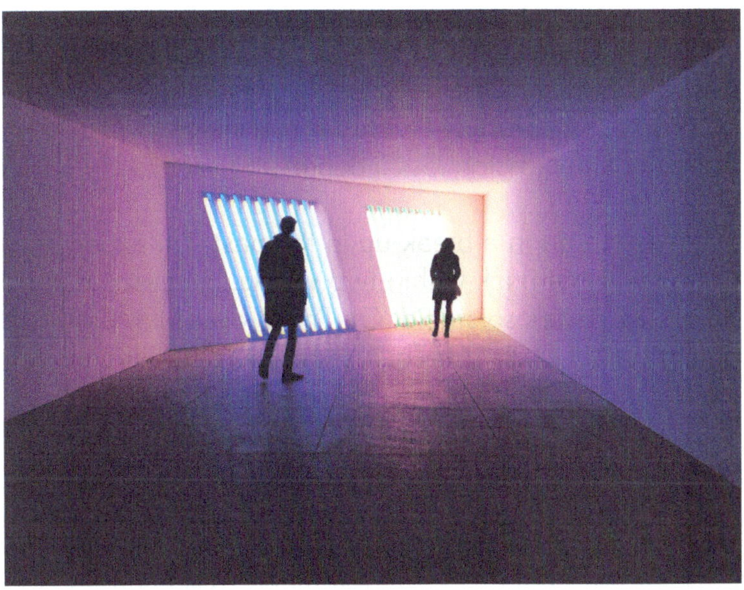

// By Elaine Huang

Opinion

Break-Up Song
// Shannon Kintner

I know by the end of the month, I'll be sick of the song. I learned the lyrics in a matter of minutes. The melancholic, calming guitar strumming, too. I came close to asking a guitar-playing friend to learn the chords so I could hear it live, but realized that I didn't want to share this song with anyone else.

This is my break-up song.

The lyrics aren't acrimonious. I passed that stage a while ago. Like, a week ago, at least. I didn't want to share this song with anyone because it's personal. The singer croons passages of my life, but it sounds pretty, so it makes this depression less... depressing.

I've been through a break-up in the past. I'm expecting to be over that prick within two weeks, because, well, his loss. Or she's so stupid. Or, I'm so over him. Or I just matured a lot faster. Or I'm just different than when we started dating. Bottom line, this should be easy, right? That prick/asshole/immature kid/lunatic/idiot will be written into the narrative of that dusty book sitting on my shelf that documents all the past "loves" of my life. In a month, this period will have an eponymous title of its own: The Benj Break-Up. My friends will know the exposition and the climax, but they won't know The Song.

My headphones shield my co-workers from knowing

that I've listened to the song even once. I disabled the Facebook sharing option on Spotify so that my friends wouldn't know how many days in a row I had listened to the same lyrics, wanting to choke my ex while at the same time wishing he would knock on my front door, rush into my office, "accidentally" bump into me downtown and proclaim his stupidity.

An hour passes. No text. No theatrical entrance, stage left, stage right. Press play.

I actually shared the song with one friend recently. "That's so sad," she replied. "Yeah, well, I'm so sad," I thought to myself. I didn't type a response. I think I just closed the Facebook tab.

My life is consumed by this break-up story right now. Soon, I will take a small step without Heartbreak. I'll realize the pernicious nature of my Song, pretending to hold my hand as I shuffle toward August, September, October. This song really just wants me to stay in June. And May. And two Marches ago. But once autumn arrives, I'll change with the leaves. I'll find a new song to listen to.

I'll forget what it was like going through a breakup. I won't reminisce on when we sat in a hammock together the first time he kissed me. The jokes about cat gifs no one else understood. The one time we accidentally crashed a funeral. I'll stop telling the story of the mountain of poison ivy we hiked for two days. That one time we thought we would run out of gas driving through Kansas. The pizza we made that was so good that we ate it standing up by the oven. I'll only remember when I started sleeping on his couch. The buckets I could have filled with nightly tears. The insecurity I felt dating someone with a better body. The fact that we never made that pizza again, even though we "had to."

I'll forget the tormented nights after "I've been thinking." I won't have dreams about "I think we should break up." And my lackluster life will find a new energy, a new beat. I'll focus my mind on things other than "I think this is for the best." A good amount of time has passed since I really did yoga consistently. I miss drinking tea instead of coffee in the morning. It's been a while since I last called, how are you doing? I decided to run a half-marathon.

And then one of my friends will find herself or himself going through a break up. He will track himself going through the five stages of grief. She won't understand the cryptic texts and emails. He can't live without him. She hates him. They don't think it's over. I won't understand why he can't just.... move on. "It's over," I'll tell them all. But this friend will have a song, and I won't know it.

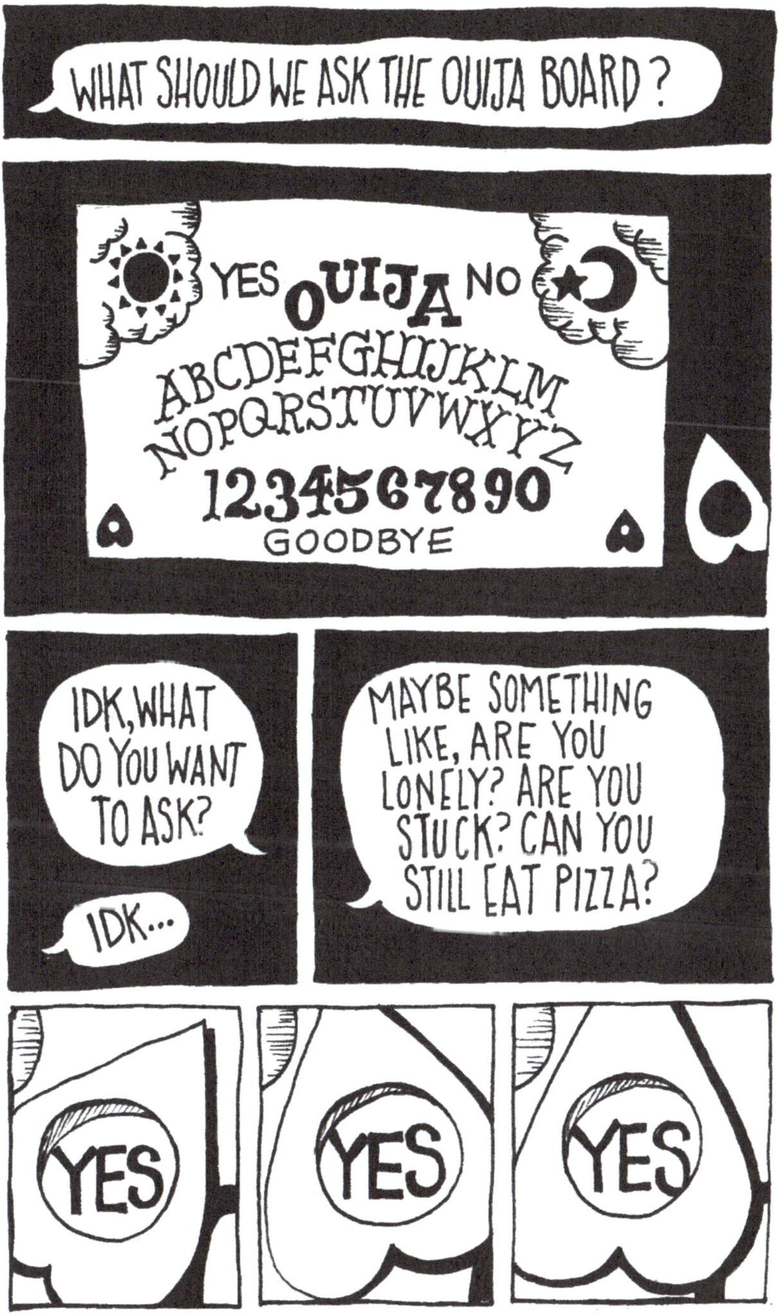

// By Jillian Barthold

Poetry

Things Age Brought Me // Savannah Monaghan

Age always hung around,
Come wind, rain; age would
Be there,
As the mark you are given at birth
With no colour or conscious.

And every day, week, year
Leaving something in my hands
That I never asked for.

Age brought me nothing I wanted.

Age brought me fifteen years of schooling,
But I still haven't learned how to forgive.

It gave me loneliness, regret and indignity
in three bottles
that I take out and sip from occasionally.

Age brought me
Three false pregnancies, but I'm still waiting
On the card that says
"Don't make the same mistake twice".

It wrapped up tolerance and handed
It to me under a table.

Age brought me fear,
And told me to always keep it
In my vision,
so I can get it before it gets me,
if it ever comes to that.

Poetry

Age brought me a blue candle
Scented with conformity.
I haven't lit it yet,
But I sometimes take it out
To display, because I've noticed
They're quite popular.

Age brought me nothing I wanted.
It said I needed
These things.

It's twenty-one years we have been together
Now, maybe this year
I will get the parcel
I asked for.

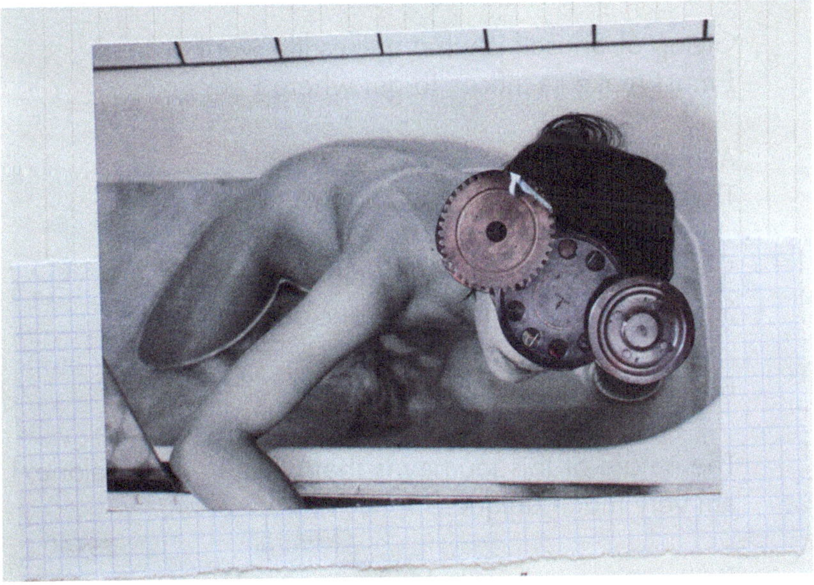

// By Amy Searle

Poetry

Repitition (Remind Me)
// Aubrie Iverson

(From that funny little gold journal, with one of those glittery Foray pens)

I am capable.

I can do all of the things that I dream of
and I can do all of the things I haven't dreamed of yet.

I am capable of becoming the person I want to be,
and the woman.

My life will not be an easy one.
The nature of life is sacrifice.

Giving of oneself is what makes life worth living.
I must make sacrifices to get where I am going.

And they will not all be martyr-worthy.
That is the worst part.

Some of them will go silent and unnoticed.
Some will become melodramatic and obnoxious.

But they are all sacrifices.

The nature of this journey is that while I am not alone, I am very much unique.

It is my uniqueness that helps me to stay afloat.

It is my uniqueness that renders me
both un-understandable

and also heartbreakingly comprehensible.

By standing out,
I blend into the crowd.

By being a part of the crowd,
I stand out.

I am not in this alone.
But I do need constant reminders that we are together.

Remind me then, when I feel lonely.
Remind me then, when rejection rears her ugly head.

Remind me, please, when the darkness comes and me
bed is cold.
Remind me then, I am not alone.

Remind me on the train, on the subway, on the bus.
Remind me at the office and when I go out for lunch.

Remind me at home
Remind me at heart

Remind me always, our powers won't part.

Remind me when I feel alone,
When I drive for miles at a time.

Remind me when I stand stock still in line.

Poetry

Remind me that power comes from the crowd
and remind me that silence often is loud.

Remind me when the paper goes to print
and instead of my own name, I see only his.

Remind me when I ask for one simple thing
that when I hear "no",

you're still on my team.

Remind me that "yes" doesn't always mean right
and remind me when I think I hear bumps in the night,

That you'll always stand by me,
not in front or behind,

because you respect me,
body and mind.

Remind me.

Thank you.

LOVELY BOUQUET

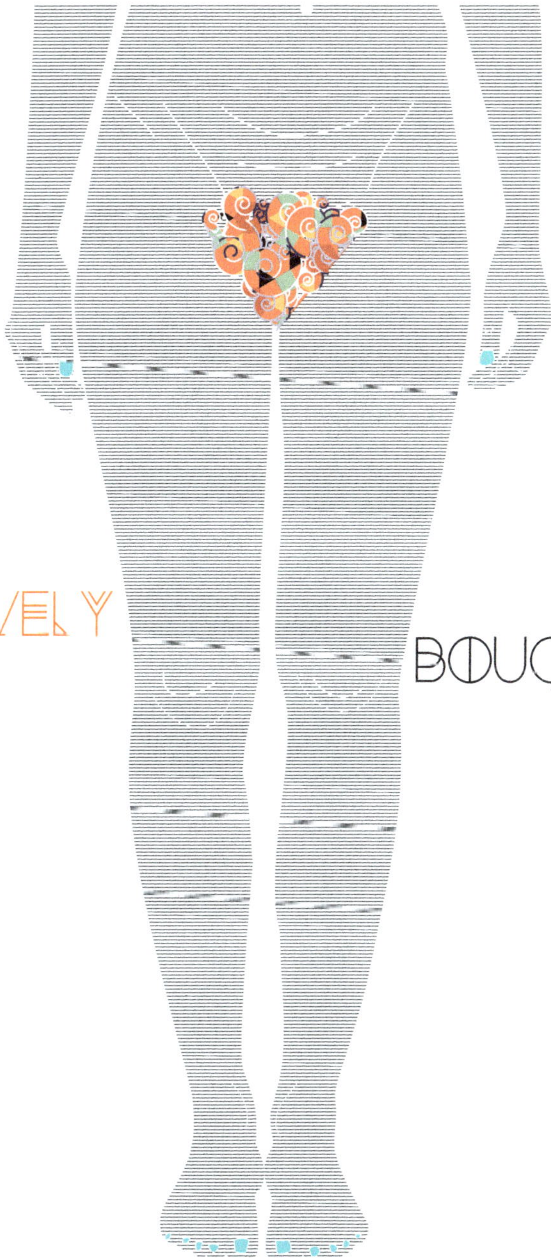

// By Savannah McAnally

Poetry

Cancer
// Caitlin Johnson

They say the ones closest to the bombs will become the air they stand in.
-Benjamin Myers

I.
He tastes like Marlboro Lights.
They all taste
like Marlboro Lights.

II.
Once upon a time,
I could say, "There are
two things running through
these veins, & neither of them
is you."

III.
I don't know who I am,
so instead I become
what other people need:
the good listener,
the dutiful girlfriend,
the whore.

IV.
Self-elision has gutted me:
dead organs overcome
by the tumor called *lovesickness*.

Untitled
// Taria Camerino

i wake
the sleeping dragon

in you

beware the flames
unbridled

all will burn

your
devout
pursuit of immunity

i do not fear the fever

only the cold ash
left behind

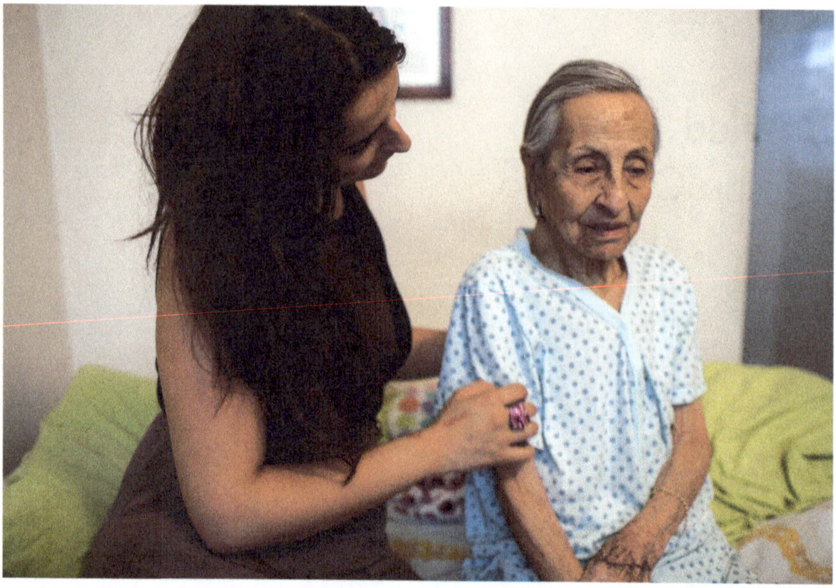

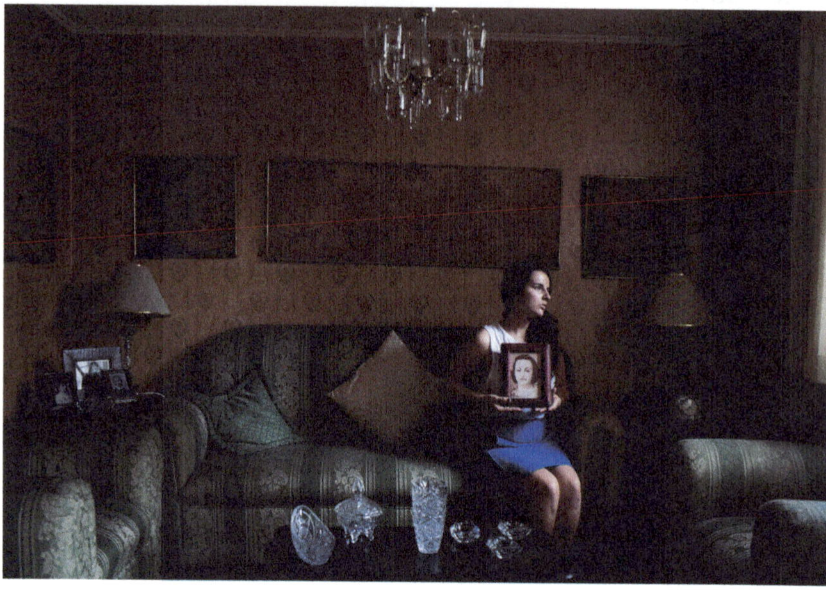

Ofelia. She is 97 and I am 24; we don't know how much longer we have.
// By Daniela Trujillo

Fatigue Tastes Like Breast Milk // April Salzano

down the throat of an infant. A sacrifice,
that until you make, you cannot claim
to know tired. You haven't even met run down,
worn out, empty, or drained until you get up
every hour and have your body emptied
in order to fill the walnut-sized stomach
of an infant. The bland, blueish fluid is not as free
as the synthetic formula pimped by the hospital,
marketed en masse, paid for by the government when what
women (or girls) have inside the pendulous decorations
they stuff inside push-up bras for the world
to gawk at, is as free as water. A bear pulled
from the sleep of hibernation by the birth
of an eight ounce cub will nurse him.
Even though she herself has not had a drop
to drink for six months, she will make him
milk. They will lay in each other's arms
until spring. He will depend on no one
but her, and she alone will make him grow,
the only formula that makes any sense.

The Coriolis Effect
// Alexa Johnson

Under the carport, I finish
my pack of cigarettes and lie
here on the cement feeling
the particles grind
against the tender places
at the back of my head,
at my shoulder blades,
and ignore the 3 a.m. siren call
urging me to put on a sweater before
my dependable wayward rotation
puts me in the wrong place,
and I consider going back
to you and getting the afghan
your mother made for our wedding,
even though it couldn't protect me
from the cold because of gaping holes,
her wide stitch.

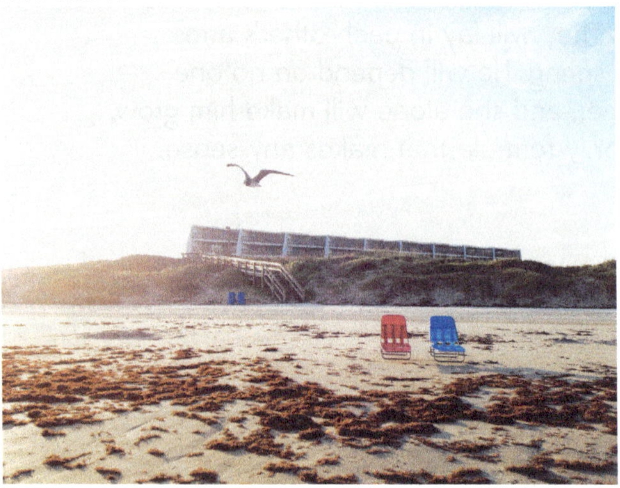

// By Elaine Huang

Fate's Intrigue
// beatjunkey

I could be intrigued
by the slightest gesture
I loiter alone
In your presence
I'm out of thought
for just a slight eternity
I silently fade to a form of melancholy
...you're so impressed
I charm you as I play
with these words to you
I cannot say
My lips so pale and exhausted
with un-flowing movement,
lying,
as I live normal
always faking
the light is not welcomed and darkness is dreaded
In between I stand
but fall
as I crash against the stars
that fell from your sky
The Stars are burning ice
from my speechless lips
And the glowing from them
Light up my eyes
luridly, fiery, and vain
...you're so inconsiderate
Place me as a void in your life
Because violated smiles will be known
There's no fate
Just truth that spoke to late.

In The End He Marries Someone Else // Lu Vola

in the original version of
the Little Mermaid, the prince marries
somebody else. the mermaid dissolves
into a pocket of sea foam on a
rocky beach, alone, unloved - except
for the sea water in which she'd been
born. it loves her so much, so unconditionally,
it absorbs her, discards her bones brittle with
unrequited love, peels away her loneliness,
reshapes her broken cells. it takes her back.

in the original story, the mermaid gives up
her tail. she gives up gliding through water
to walk on the hard, unforgiving earth, which is so
painful it feels like walking on glass shards.

this is what makes the prince love her.
the fact that her constant pain makes her
so graceful. she treads ground so lightly,
like she does not belong. as if at any time,
the ground beneath her will grow a mouth
and swallow her up.

but what i really mean is that what the prince
really loved was her fear. her unconditional love
for him was just a bonus, vying for his affection,
mutilating her body, growing limbs that punished her.
for him, she inhabited a body
that was not hers.
left her home.

learned how to walk
instead of swim.
lost her voice so that
she could not argue.

as if we can buy love with sacrifices.
as if we can earn it through pain.

in the end, he still
marries someone else.

i will tell my daughter: this is the fairytale closest to
reality. one day you will fall in love with a boy.
you will change for him. dye your hair, starve your
body, pack suitcases, live in sad apartments across
the country, and do things you said you'd never do.
like beg for him to love you. leave your door
unlocked just in case he decides to come back.
never mind the draft he might bring inside with
him, or the questionable, absent nights.
never mind that he has snuffed out the lights
that once burned from inside your eyes.

you are a mermaid without your tail
walking on a ground of hot coals.
your life will become one long wince.
holding your breath, praying for the day
you will get to keep him.

but in the end,
he still marries someone else.

and i hope your sacrifices will not
have been too great. i hope the sea

will forgive you. take you back into
its gritty arms, and at first you won't realize
- see, you've lived with saltwater
on your lips for so long to know the difference.
but then you'll know. you'll notice the absence
of pain. feel the ache in your bones wash away.
your last breath will be a sigh of relief
that will roll over like early morning fog
on an empty beach.

he will marry someone else, i know,
but don't worry. because the worst
that can happen is that it will
finally set you free.

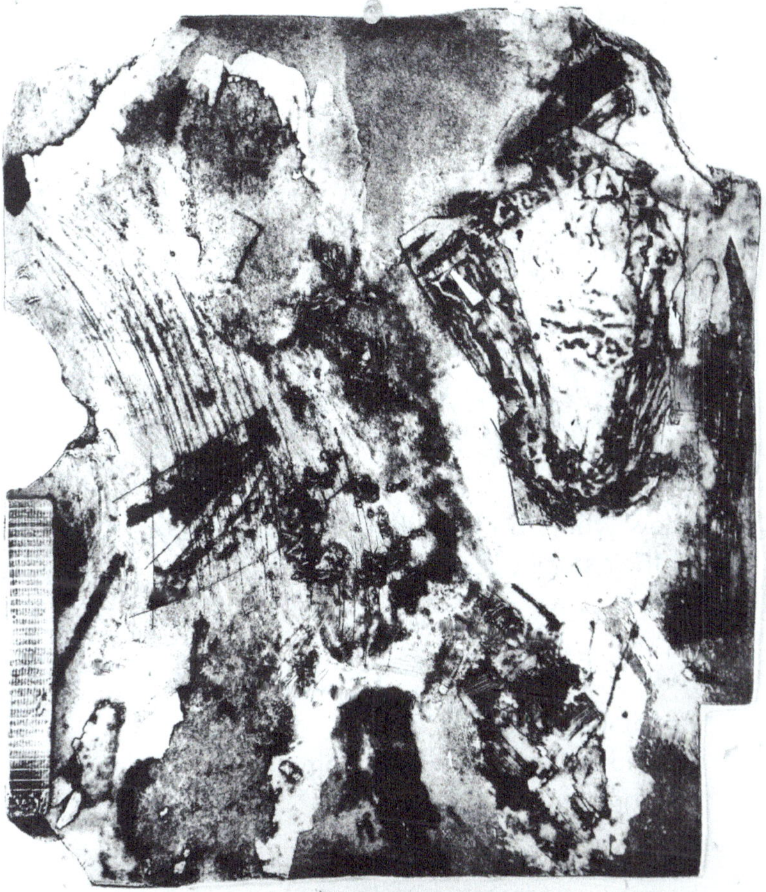

// By Kendal Kulley

Haikus About The Future
// Nicole Stewart

I dream of puppies,
connectedness, fresh veggies
and a new sofa

+

We can do more good
in the world if we don't care
who gets the credit

+

Do caterpillars
know what's on the other side
of their small cocoons?

+

Reading before bed
tucked between the lines I am
drifting off to sleep

Twisting & Spilling
// Christian Ryan Criswell

my head is the rock
and my heart is the hard place
my eyes and mouth
stuck stoically in between
my tongue twisting
and spilling
illogical reasoning
and my brain isn't sleeping
cause it's always open
constantly glowing like a 24-hour wal-mart
with its fbrescent lights
always humming and buzzing
and my thoughts
are pacing around the isles
and stopping halfway
like they are high and forgot
why they came in the first place
but they've got nothing better to do
so they just keep browsing
and fantasizing about the life they could be having
and after a while of wondering
they're stuck standing at the self-checkout line
with its beep beep beep beep
reminding me that i need a machine to make my heart beat
and how it has been silently soaking up concrete
and now its texture consists of imprints of all the feet
that have walked all over the once soft surface
while it was still malleable and forming
the occasional weed pushes through the cracks
in search of sunlight
and wilts and the sight

of my dark insides
the hollow echo of my soul unsung
reverberates in my black lungs
all those ashes
all those lives
sucked up and stomped out like a simple cigarette
and sometimes my hard as rock thoughts
get to shifting, softening, thinking
some adventure enthusiast
might want to take the plunge
and spelunk down into the depths
with only a match and a slice of hope
picking away at the tiny pebbles
praying to eventually see
the pumping organ
beating, breathing, flowing with blood
hinting at the capacity to love
but exhaustion sets in so soon
and the reasoning for the hide and seek search
for proof of my soul
dissolves
so they boarded up the doors and windows
and put up a barricade on a one way street
so it's clear to see it's impossible to get to me
and i have loved and accepted myself inside out
and learned to stop expecting the same from anyone else

I Am Accidental

// A.J. Huffman

wish, a mistake manifested
by a trio of rubs and a slip of semantics.
I am not the genie you hoped for,
but rather the apparition you are stuck with.
I am prisoner of your selfishly constructed penitentiary.
I am weary of your corners and wearing thin
haunting their shadows. I am intoxicating
myself into oblivion. Intentionally
pretending I am still sealed inside anonymous bottle. Locked
under glass and cork, I am dreaming
of airless breathing, of returning to century's sleep.

// By Amy Searle

Poetry

I Am A Motherless Daughter // Kimberly Worthington

My mother is a tall brunette, she used to dye her hair a glossy, deep, and radiant red.
My mother is an introvert, who embodied her independence by taking care of her family.
My mother has a smile big and heart-shaped that is incomparable to anything.
My mother is patient and forgiving, to a fault.
My mother is worried, anxious, seeking control of her own life; confused by what it means to be true to your dreams and be the leader of others' lives.
My mother is a beautiful woman, who held hardship like I never could imagine.
My mother died October 4, 2013.

I am a tall brunette, growing my hair long and towards the ground.
I am an introvert, who devotes her life to teaching young children pride and self-awareness.
I have a smile big, heart-shaped, and teethy.
I am patient and forgiving, but to forget is something I have yet to conquer.
I am heartbroken, lonely, and grasping for control; confused by my reality.
I am a beautiful woman, taught to be strong by my mother.
I am a motherless daughter, sad and longing for the lessons I had yet to learn.

Untitled
// Samantha Johnson

call me rose water, for i am her
i travel where i fit
slip through lustful fingers
right when you thought your
tips were sticky enough
to tame me

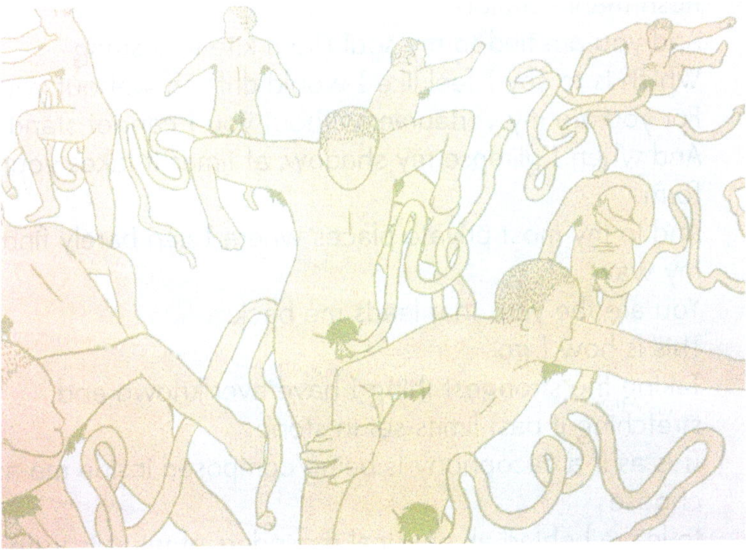

// By Olivia Kates

Poetry

Breadcrumbs
// Quinn MaBelle

I go, your love sewn into the hem of my fingers,
Your laugh stowed in the folds of my arms,
your tears watering the roots of my legs, I go.
I go.
I go and you do not follow, at least not in the material way.
I go and you travel along in my body
You come along in my body because my soul has a flesh manifestation
And you are tied to my soul like a kite to a string
Which is to say I feel like I would drift off without you.
For you are my vertebrae, without you I cannot stand
And when I glimpse my shadow, at times it takes your form
And in my most private places where I can barely find my way
You are the yarn that leads me back.
This is how I go
Taking the strongest thing I have ever known and stretching it past limits set in stone
It is as if a cacophony is being composed inside me as I choose
to leave behind all physical reminders of what is truth in my spirit, I go
and I take what you've helped me become, I go and I take you with me.
I take you with me partly in fear, do I know how to live without you?
Near me in the night or spontaneous phone calls and those

Sun dipped summer afternoons when we listened to
music that cooled our disappointment
making us one with our heartbeat.
Those memories spilt on the earth from here to San
Marcos
A trail of pandulce and breadcrumb memories for the
birds to ingest
Taking our bond and using it to fly
I have cried wondering at how I am to live without you
Forgetting those times when I already have survived to
find our love again in a new way
There have been days I have lived in myself so strongly
I shed every last scale of my frightened and needy skin.
Days where I inhabited my life in totality
And those days I felt more appreciative of you than ever
Because we were sharing our wholes instead of
mending our halves.
As I go I take myself and I take yourself too
As I go I trust our bond will continue
I go, blessing, honoring, cherishing
I go, believing that as I grow you will grow too.
I go, hoping you remember how I love you.

Poetry

Ode To My Mother
// Lu Vola

every time i taste the bile
filling my mouth at the mention
of my own mother, i remember
the scar that runs along her stomach.
she is a road map made frail with creases
and it is a highway that cuts her
perfectly in half. it is the Mississippi,
dried out. and i am the boat that docked
and never looked back.

it is a fact that
it was i who ruined her
once-perfect, shapely body.

i wonder if she remembers
the feeling of being sliced open
every time i clench my fists
and think to myself that if i tell her
that i hate her, it would be the same as
gutting open my own veins and drowning
my bone marrow with gasoline. i would be
bludgeoning the hands that raised me.
that held me when my every thought
still revolved around when i was going to
be held next.

(it was so simple. sometimes i
try to de-evolve, to need her
in that way again. i dig through
the trash for my umbilical cord,

to reattach. do you remember when
you used to cry when your mother
left the room?

when will be the next time?
in a hospital room astringent with regret,
blood racing to the screech of
a flat line?)

i rose from my mother
the way a flower rises from
the dirt. my mother is the rain.
she is the thunder and the flood.
but she is the sun, too.
the giving soil.

i scarred a mark on her.
she scarred her soul in me.

my mother is in my cells.
so when i say i hate her,
i mean to say, i hate me,
too.

Style

Sweet Spring Picks // Olive & Myrtle

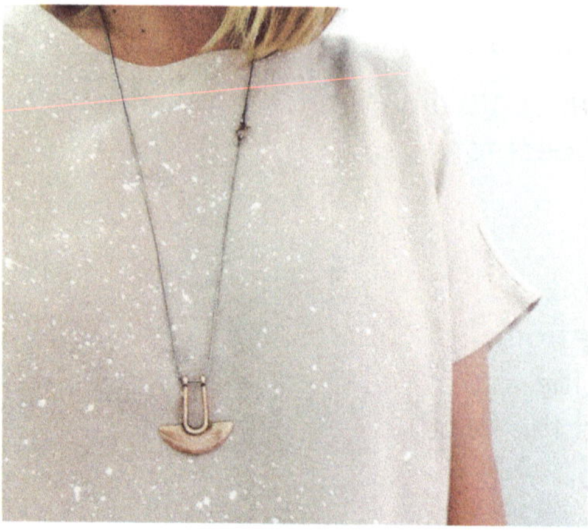

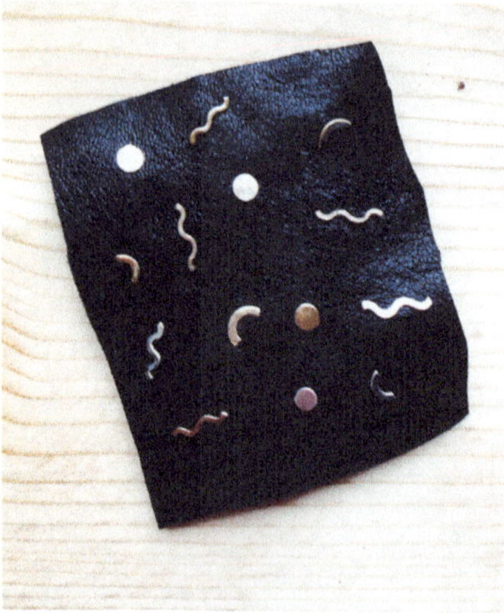

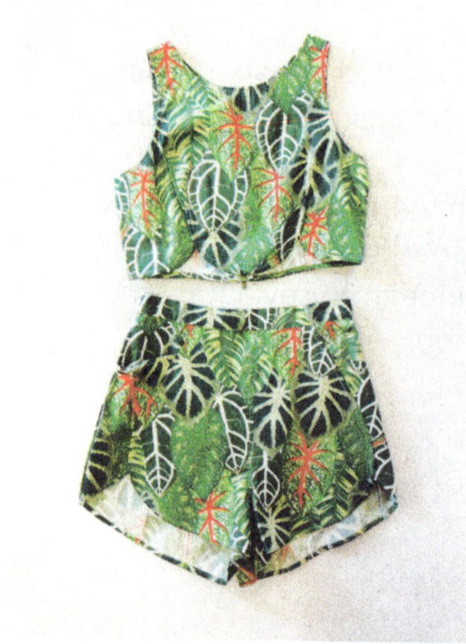

Olive's Favourites by Laura Uhlir

Samantha Pleet Fauna Leaf Tank & Shorts:
I'm crazy about this tropical print from Samantha Pleet -- I can't decide if I like it better in the tank or the shorts. Despite their cropped length, both pieces are insanely flattering!

Evens Sand Linen Box Top & Tiro Tiro Quarta Necklace:
I love this minimal linen top from up and coming Texas designer Evens. It feels just right for Spring layering and it'll surely keep you cool in the dog days of Summer. Teaming it up with Portland jewelry favorite Tiro Tiro is just gravy.

Hey Murphy Confetti Studs:
I've been following Texas jewelry designer Hey Murphy's work for ages and every time I think her work couldn't get better, it does! Her latest batch of single stud earrings is the perfect mix of minimalism and whimsy.

Style

Baggu Leather Drawstring Bucket Bag:
Baggu can do no wrong in my eyes and their leather drawstring bucket bag is just about my favorite piece of theirs. Buttery leather, classic construction, warm caramel-y color -- this bag's a winner.

Skargorn #61 Tee:
Skargorn tees. Skargorn tees! Skargorn teeeees! Can you tell I love these guys? Do yourself a favor and scoop up one of these USA made guys in every color. Their durable construction, easy oversized fit, and nice details (hey, notched collar and ever-so-slightly scooped neckline) will keep them in constant closet rotation.

Ilana Kohn Sammet Dress:
Well hey there, cutest floral print I've ever seen! Ilana Kohn, a commercial illustrator turned fashion designer, has quickly made herself a name as the go-to lady for effortless cool-girl pieces in classic cuts & whimsical prints. This dreamboat of a dress is no exception.

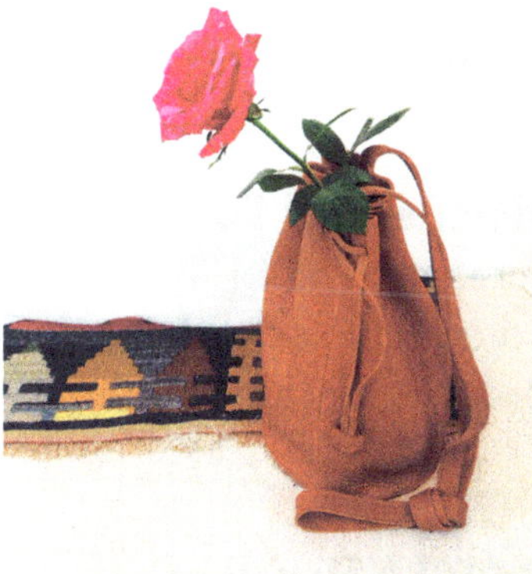

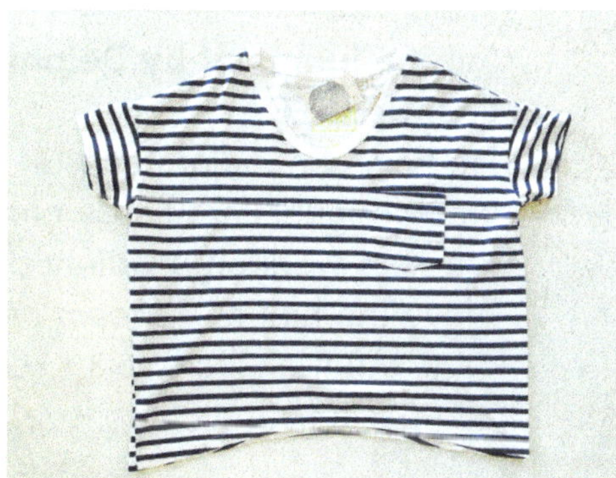

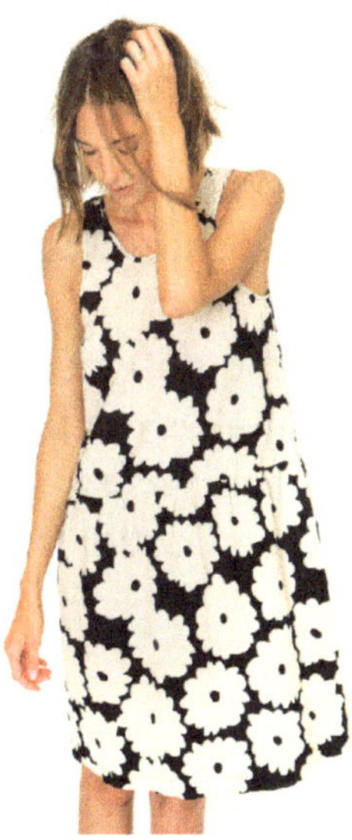

Myrtle's Favourites by Whitney Bickers

Sail dress by Filly (Emily Christensen of Portland):
You can never go wrong with cream linen for the Spring or Summer and I like how this dress acts as a clean slate for your own style, whether ultra girly vintage or stark minimalism.

Sabine jumpsuit by Delphine (Yuka Itsuzu of Pasadena, CA):
I'm having a major jumpsuit moment this Spring! I'm glad designers are finally embracing them in new shapes that can work on a variety of heights and body types. I love the hint of *I Dream of Jeannie* in this elastic cuff pant, but the Liberty print keeps it classic and modern. Add pockets and I'm in love.

Borrower's Blouse & Keplar trousers by Feral Childe (Moriah Carlson of Brooklyn, NY & and Alice Wu of Oakland, CA):
I like doing mixed prints from the same designer -- it's a little safer on matching tones but makes me feel like a style genius. A new print always feels fresh in your closet, but switch to boots and you can count this as a fall investment as well.

Style

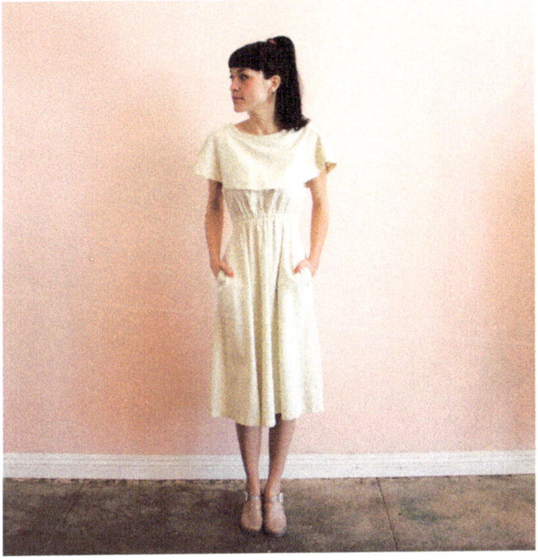

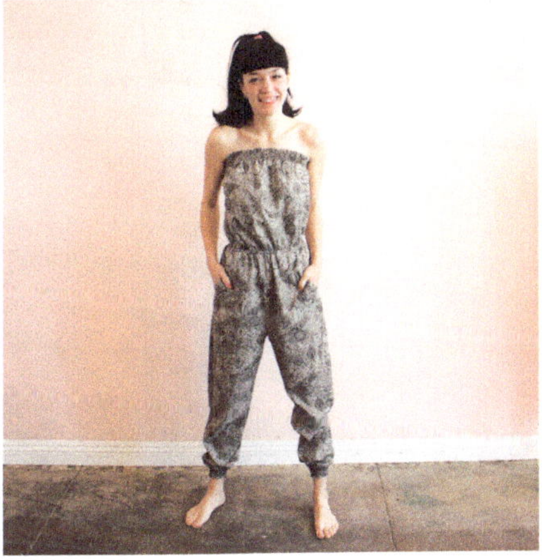

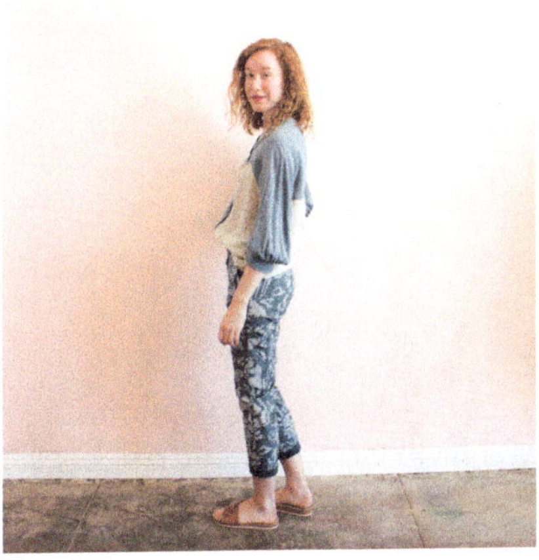

Style

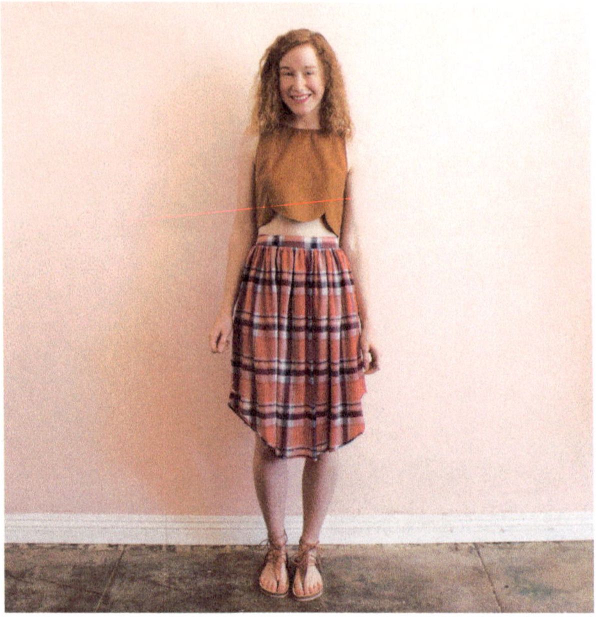

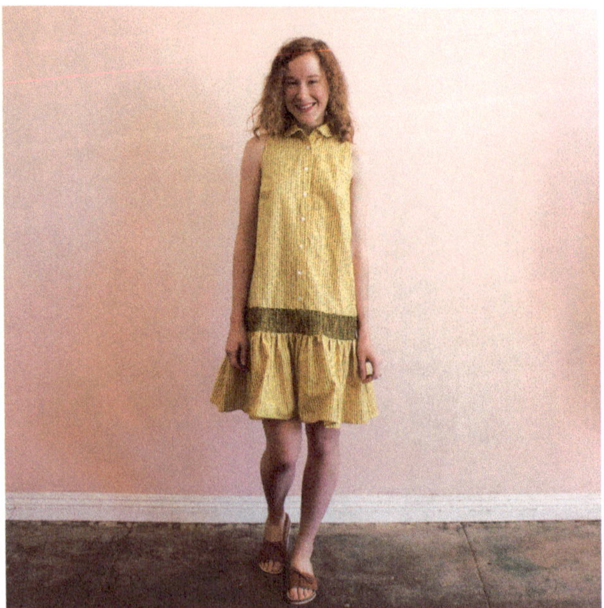

Leaf top by Samantha Pleet (New York) and Tara skirt by Stella Proseyn (Debbie Talanian of Los Angeles, CA):
This Summer I'm vowing to get over my body issues -- or at least work on them a little. High-waist skirts with tees are practically a uniform for me, so I'm easing myself into midriff territory with this crop top that doesn't bare too much.

Boscobel smocked dress by Thomas Sires (Fiona Thomas and Allison Sires of New York):
Bright and festive colors are calling to me for Spring -- especially since I'm planning a Mexico honeymoon this Summer! An easy washable cotton dress is just the thing for hot days and gorging on tacos

My Room // Sara Hollis

Moving to a new city far away from family and friends is not easy. I knew from the very beginning that I wanted to put extra thought into my new space in order to make me feel as comfortable as possible in my new environment.

Most importantly, my bedroom is a place where I can un-wind after a busy day at work. On the weekends, it is a space where I can spend time alone and feel at ease while enjoying coffee and a good book. My main goal was to make the space functional yet simple, minimal yet inspiring.

A spacious living area is hard to come by in this city, and my place is no exception. Luckily, I have three large bay windows that open up the space and provide an incredible view of my neighborhood. I have very thin curtains to allow for as much light as possible -- my favorite thing is waking up in the morning to the sunlight! Since I often don't need much additional light, I replaced the old light fixture with a vintage Edison bulb pendant that gives a dim glow in the evening.

In order to keep the space minimalistic and de-cluttered, I stuck with mostly whites and light woods, with a little splash of color with a bright rug and a few music posters and prints that I had snagged from various shows and museums.

My garment rack (where I hang my favorite coats) and my wooden bike stand allow me to store these items in a way that saves space yet add their own flare.

I spend a lot of time writing to friends and family across the country, and I love pinning up my postcards I have received -- both as a daily reminder and a simple decoration.

Most of my furniture I found from vintage shops in my neighborhood, and I enjoy getting fresh flowers and succulents from the local Mission shops every now and again as a fun addition.

Overall, my bedroom has been my safe haven amidst the craziness of this wonderful city. It's a perfect place to retreat to and re-energize for the day ahead!

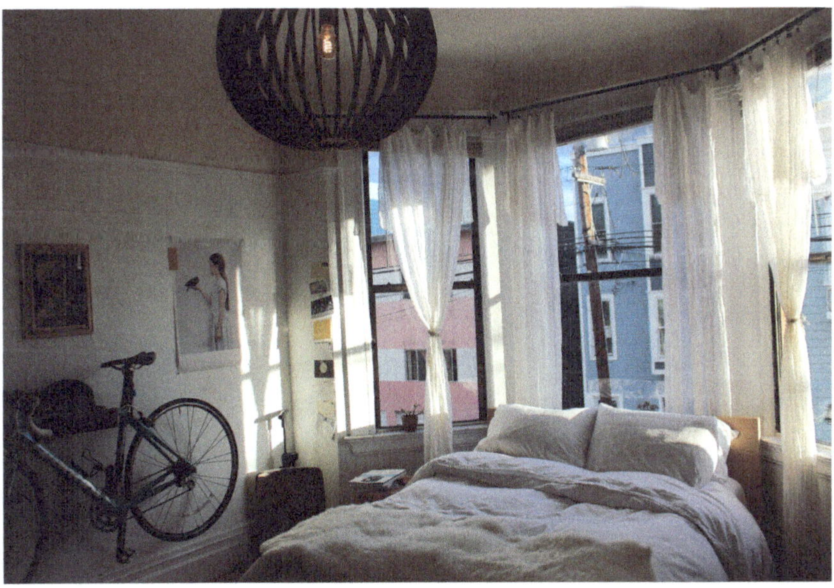

Music

SXSW Music Favourites
// Hillary-Anne Crosby

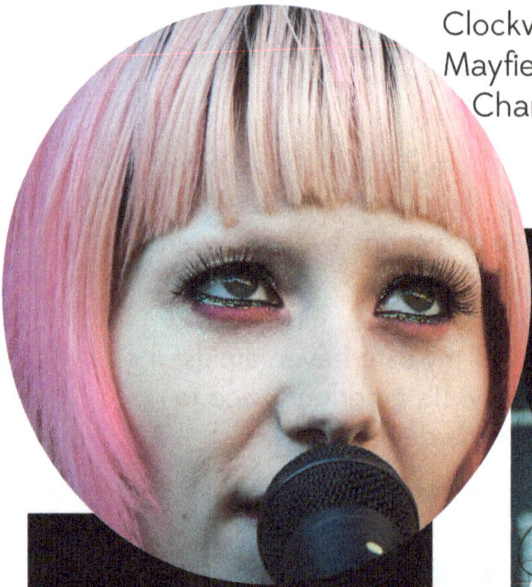

Clockwise: Jessica Lea Mayfield, Dum Dum Girls, Charli XCX, Denitia and sene.

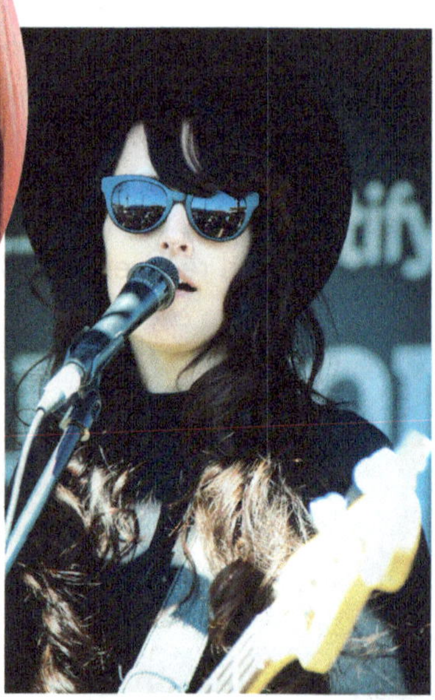

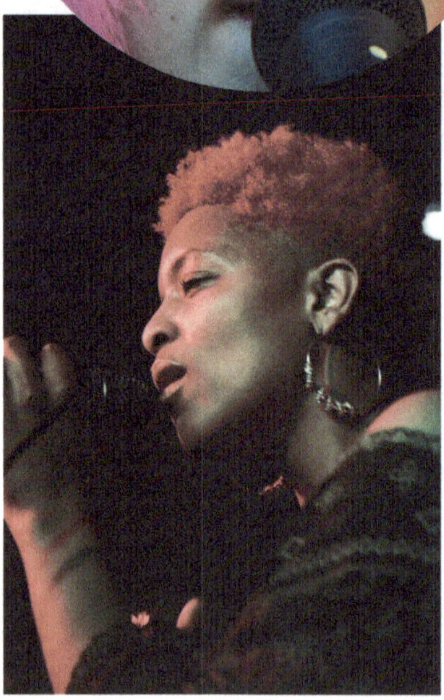

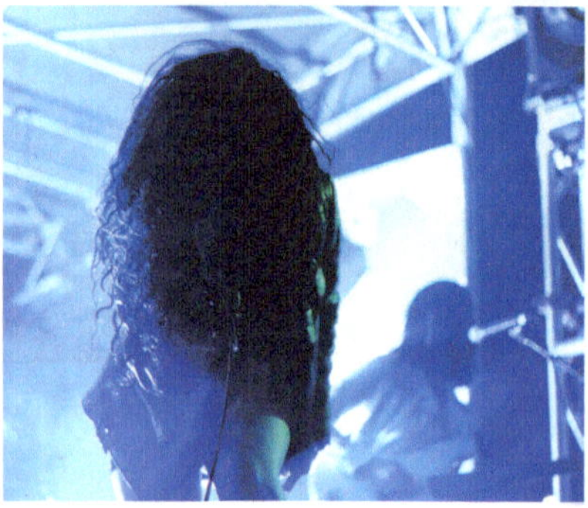

Music

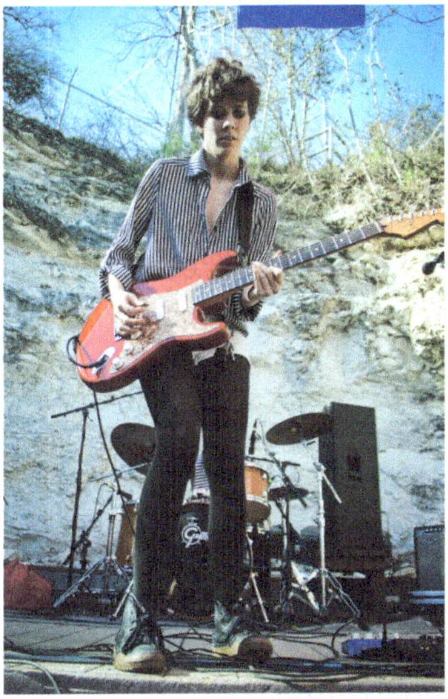

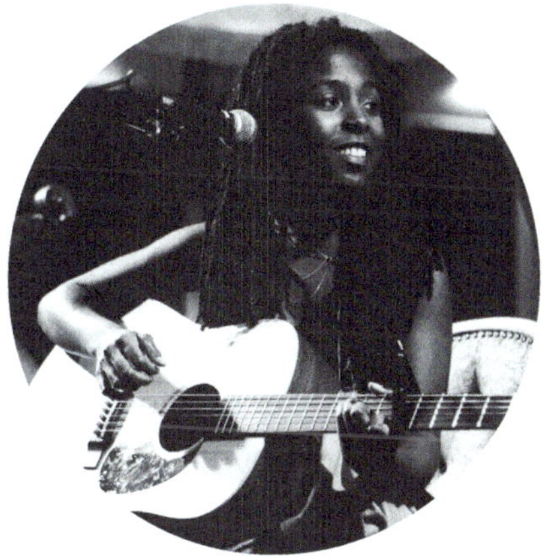

Clockwise: Aisha Burns, Those Darlins, Wye Oak, Ex Hex

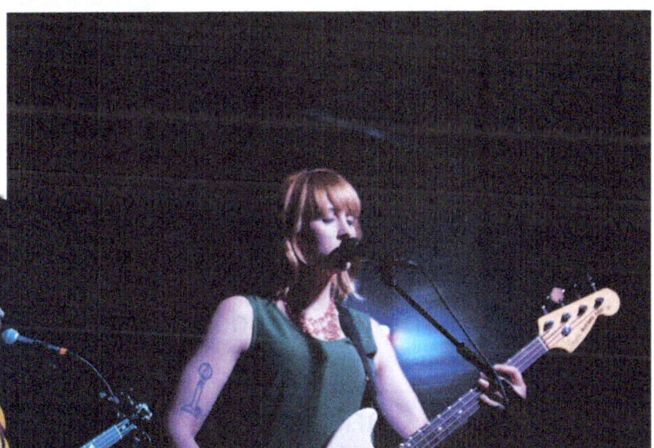

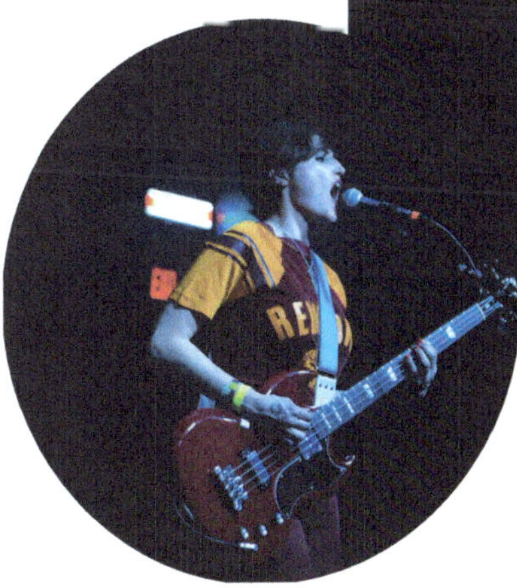

Film

My SXSW Film Top 5 // Hillary-Anne Crosby

1. Fort Tilden

Two girls reminding us that the struggle is real and lady-led comedies are the best? Yes and please. I started laughing thirty seconds in and never really stopped. Highly recommended for anyone who likes (but maybe doesn't love) HBO's Girls.

2. Veronica Mars

I'm not even going to explain this one. It's gosh darn Veronica Mars, y'all.

3. Beyond Clueless

An incredibly look at the high school movies we came of age with and how they helped us understand ourselves, our peers, and our raging hormones.

4. Vessel

Women on Waves have worked to provide off-shore abortions and advice since 2000. This documentary is a look at the ups and downs and whys and hows.

5. Wild Canaries

This comedy-noir mash-up was a real treat; I laughed so hard that suspenseful scenes caught me off guard, and even those were worth laughing through. Added bonus: Sophia Takal and Alia Shawkat as the leading ladies.

About

Kathryn Bailey is a 22-going-on-75 year old writer. She has a degree in creative writing from the University of Missouri and loves dogs, whiskey, TV, and breakfast tacos. She tweets at @ kaaathyyy. [Dallas, Texas]

Jillian Barthold is an illustrator and designer currently living with two super cool humans and three sassy cats. She enjoys staring at the moon, sitting in the ocean, marathoning television shows, and a light hearted game of pinball. You can check out her work at MonsterSongs.tumblr.com and contact her anytime at Jillian.Barthold@gmail.com. [Chicago, Illinois]

Whitney Bickers opened Myrtle in 2011 as a place to gather independent female designers from around the world. The shop is a brick & mortar boutique in the Echo Park neighborhood. [Los Angeles, California]

Basia Borodziewicz is a proud Polish-Texan, Arabic speaking feminist who likes her days sunny, her food spicy, and her travel frequent. [Plano, Texas]

Tarla Camerino is so much; the hardest part is just knowing what order to put them in partner, mother, radical, candy maker, pastry chef, writer, designer. [Gainesville, Florida]

Christian Ryan Criswell is a writer and photographer who wants to say yes with you! Find out more at Say Yes Austin on Facebook & Twitter. [Austin, Texas]

Hillary-Anne Crosby is founder and editor-in-chief of *Vagina*. She's slowly working on a book about lady cyclists, reading Anna Karenina for the tenth time, and trying to build a life around working with and for women. [Austin, Texas]

About

Becky Lee Flores began writing poetry in 1994 and attended Cottey College, all-girls private college where she studied Journalism and English. Published by 'Who's Who in Poetry' and 'Poetry.com' as a teen, she continues to publish poetry today as beatjunkey.
[Austin, Texas]

Sara Hollis graduated from the University of Texas where she studied Business, Pre-med, and African Studies. Upon graduation she moved to San Francisco where she works for a coffee roasting company and helps run a non-profit focused on international development. Aside from work and drinking lots of good coffee, she loves bicycle adventures with her beloved Bianchi, meeting new friends, and Siracha sauce. [San Francisco, California]

Elaine Huang is a true native Austinite, a rare find these days, just like unicorns. She loves photography and how it holds a different meaning for each person who holds the camera. You can see stories unfold and enter a whole new world by looking through the lens of another photographer. [Austin, Texas]

A.J. Huffman has published seven solo chapbooks and one joint chapbook through various small presses. Her eighth solo chapbook, Drippings from a Painted Mind, won the 2013 Two Wolves Chapbook Contest. She is a Pushcart Prize nominee, and her poetry, fiction, and haiku have appeared in hundreds of national and international journals. She is also the founding editor of Kind of a Hurricane Press. www.kindofahurricanepress.com [Ormond Beach, Florida]

Aubrie Iverson is an aspiring journalist currently working on an undergraduate degree from Texas State University and writing as a trends reporter for the student paper, The University Star. She cherishes music, literature and all of the arts, and hopes to eventually make a career out of writing about artists and their work. [San Marcos, Texas]

Alexa Johnson believes in the power of comprehensive sex education, vintage furs, and late night sweat. She is partial to hot sauce and cooperative living. [Erie, Pennsylvania]

Caitlin Johnson is the Managing Editor of CAIRN: The St. Andrews Review. Her work has appeared in All Things Girl, Black Mirror Magazine, Charlotte Viewpoint, Fortunates, Pembroke Magazine, and What the Fiction, among other outlets. [Detroit, Michigan]

Samantha Johnson has been writing since she could pick up a pen and loves to travel and explore the million different facets of life. She's originally from the Bay Area in California and will be moving to NYC this year. You can learn more about her at srosej.com. [California

Olivia Kates is a current sophomore at RISD majoring in printmaking and adding elements of textile and fiber arts to her practice. Her work directly addresses or stems from issues of gender, race and subculture. [Providence, Rhode Island]

Shannon Kintner works for food magazine Edible Austin as Marketing Assistant. She is also a freelance photographer. [Austin, Texas]

Kendal Kulley enjoys watching plastic bags dance. She's interested in how beings interact with one another and the dynamics of those relations. She makes prints and she make a lot of other things. [Austin, Texas]

About

Courtney Leigh likes to read books and write things. She also makes music with The Villettes. Find her here: @CourtLeighLove. [Austin, Texas]

Quinn MaBelle is a queer, bi-racial, white passing, gender fluid female who writes poetry to get through the day. She is currently studying at Texas State University San Marcos to become a therapist specializing in the treatment of eating disorders within the queer/poc community. [San Marcos, Texas]

Savannah Anatoli McAnally is a Graphic Designer. She's the Co-Founder and Design Editor of a feminist compilation zine, Heroine Zine. [Austin, Texas]

Savannah Monaghan is twenty-one and studying creative writing and art history at the University of Melbourne. [Melbourne, Australia]

Recently nominated for two Pushcart Prizes, **April Salzano** teaches college writing in Pennsylvania where she lives with her husband and two sons. She has finished her first collection of poetry and is working on a memoir on raising a child with autism. The author also serves as co-editor at Kind of a Hurricane Press. [New Castle, Pennsylvania]

Amy Searle has a BFA in Photography from Texas State University and an itch to explore and experience. She loves capturing as well as re-creating details and memories from moments in her life. [San Marcos, Texas]

Nicole Stewart is a soon-to-be graduate of The University of Texas in Austin. The first thing she plans to do when she finds a job with her shiny new advertising degree is adopt a beagle. [Austin, Texas]

About

Daniela Trujillo was born in Medellin, Colombia. 39 countries and still counting. She puts her face in the birthday cakes. She was always the one to break the piñatas. Together is all she is after. [Stockholm, Sweden]

Laura Uhlir is a photographer, stylist, and vintage collector. Her shop Olive features a stock carefully curated independent design as well as a selection of hand picked, timeless vintage classics. It is a space to discover new work and re-discover old favorites. [Austin, Texas]

Lu Vola is a lover of words and coffee. You can find her art and poetry chapbooks at etsy.com/shop/artschoolbully. [San Diego, California]

Bee Walsh is a New York native living in Bedford-Stuyvesant. Twenty five years old, Internet Coquette & Poetry Editor at The Rain, Party, & Disaster Society, published here and there, trying different cities on for size. [New York, New York]

You will likely find **Kimberly Worthington** devouring a book, watching a cheesy movie, slurping on some dark coffee and sporting her newly gifted ice-cream cone earrings. [Austin, Texas]

About

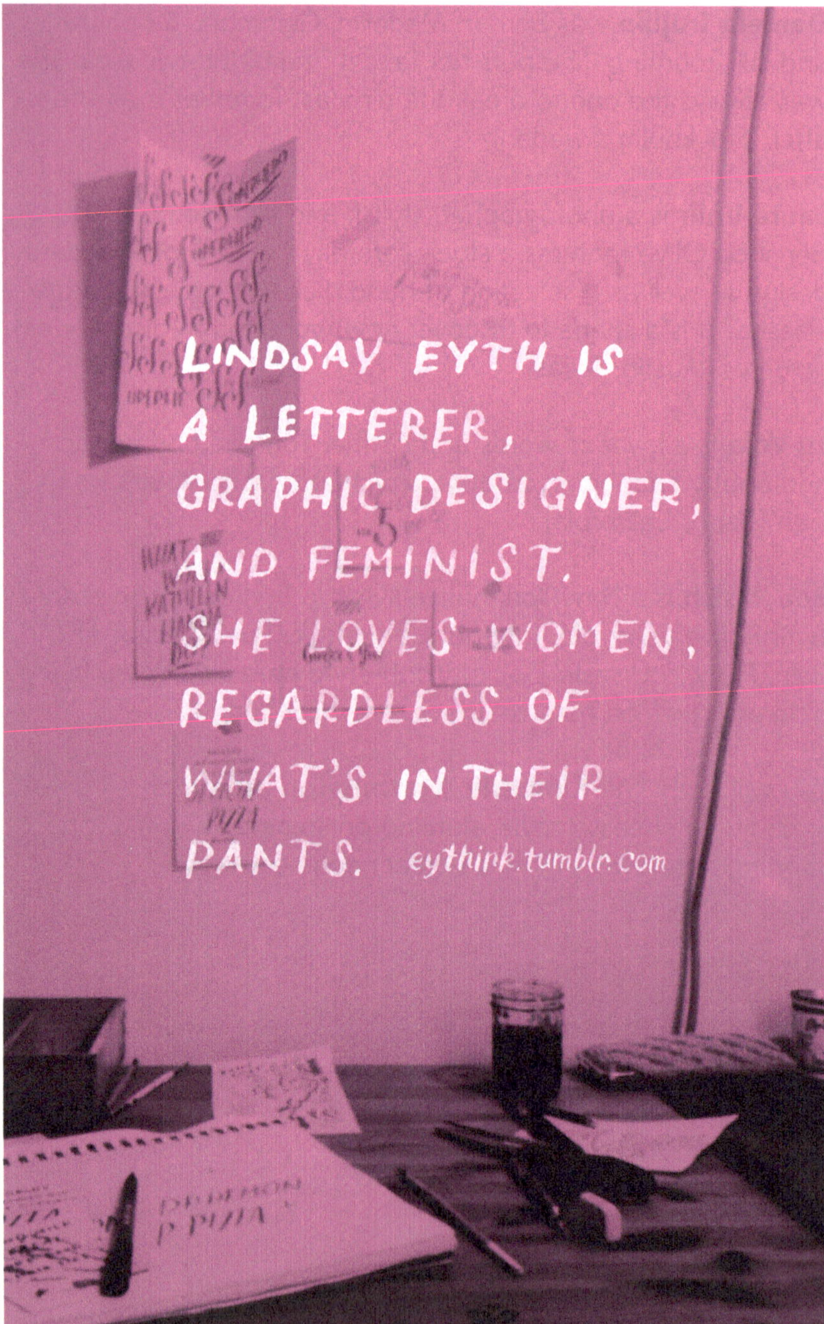
LINDSAY EYTH IS
A LETTERER,
GRAPHIC DESIGNER,
AND FEMINIST.
SHE LOVES WOMEN,
REGARDLESS OF
WHAT'S IN THEIR
PANTS.
eythink.tumblr.com

About

Valerie and Paula Wolf are the sisters behind Davy Gray, a creative company offering floral design and photography services. More of their work can be found at davygray.com

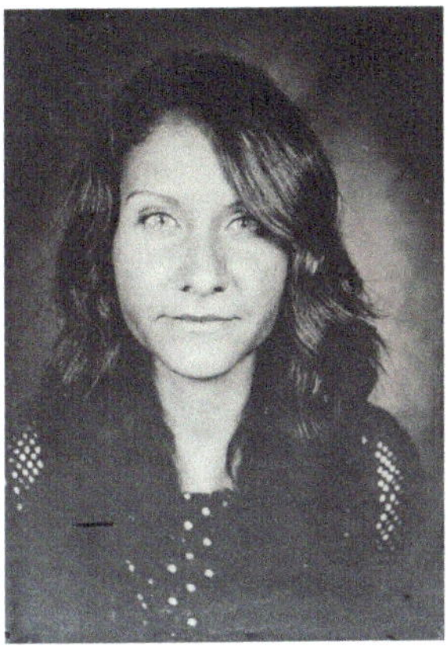
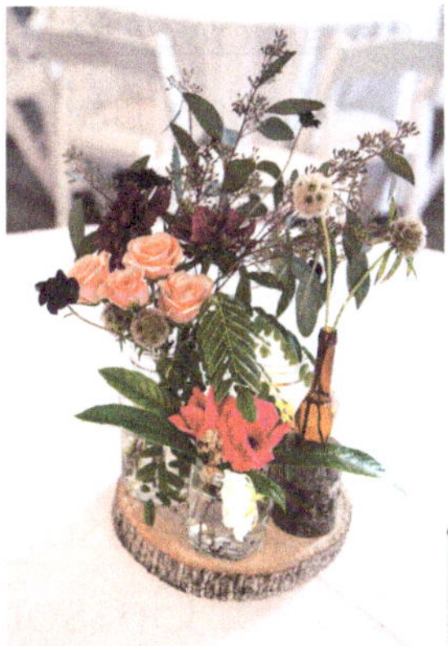
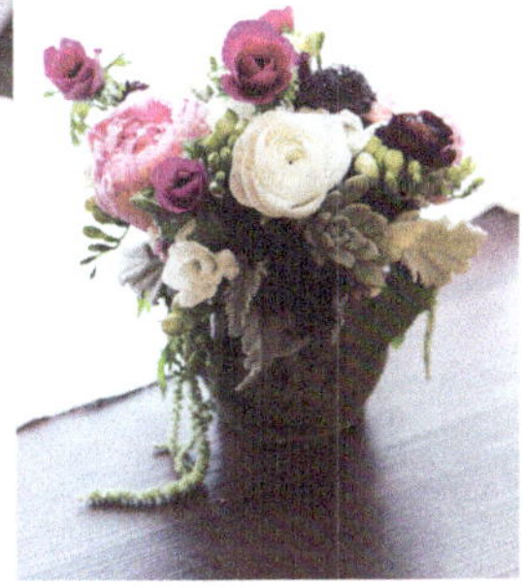

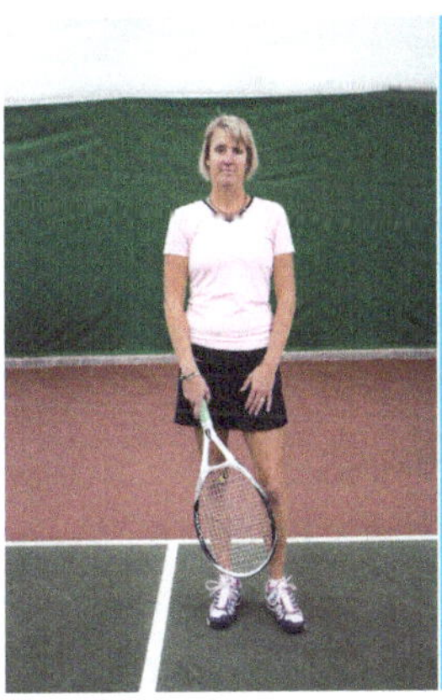
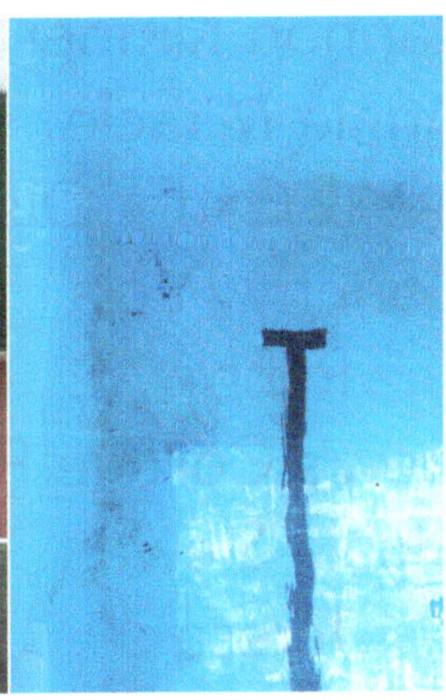
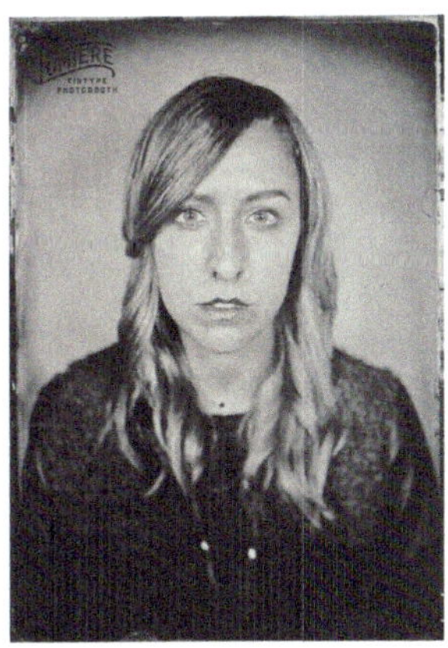

Thank You

V-Scouts

Thank you to everyone who backed

Vagina's Spring '14 Kickstarter campaign!

Including:

Kassy Balli
Alex Bohs
Basia Borodziewicz
Christina
Rachel Gilbert
Karl Gossot
Lisa J. Grissom
Marta Hinkle
Carlyn Hudson
Alexa Johnson
Shannon Kintner
Angie Miracle
Heather & Carter Olson
Johnny Pacia
Robby
St. Andrew's College Press
Nicole Stewart
Teresa
Victoria Vassileva
VM
Kristin L. Ware
Sarah E. Williams

Thank You

olive

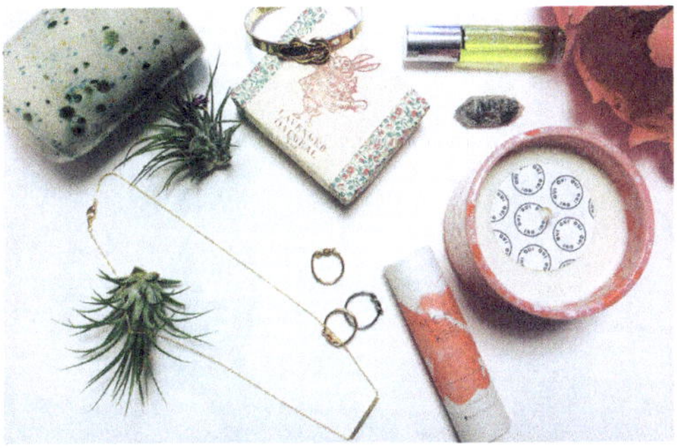

timeless vintage ○ thoughtful design

1223 ROSEWOOD AVE, AUSTIN TX   WWW.OLIVEAUSTIN.COM

MANTIS
MASSAGE

Thank You

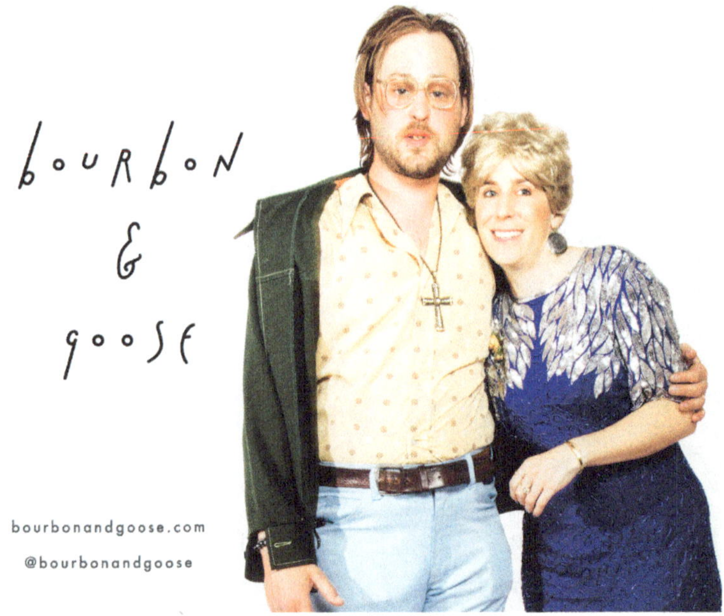
bourbon
&
goose
bourbonandgoose.com
@bourbonandgoose

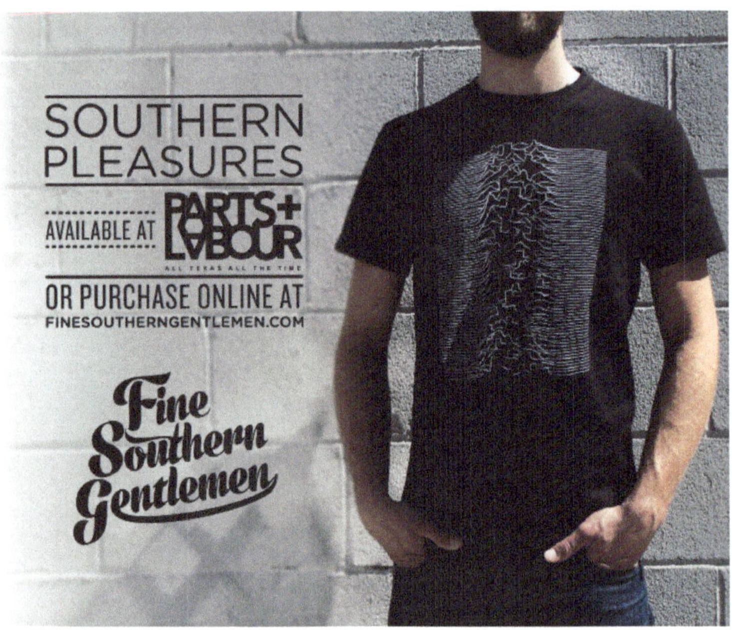
SOUTHERN
PLEASURES
AVAILABLE AT PARTS + LABOUR
ALL TEXAS ALL THE TIME
OR PURCHASE ONLINE AT
FINESOUTHERNGENTLEMEN.COM
Fine
Southern
Gentlemen

Thank You

WUNDER-PILZ
· KOMBUCHA TEA ·

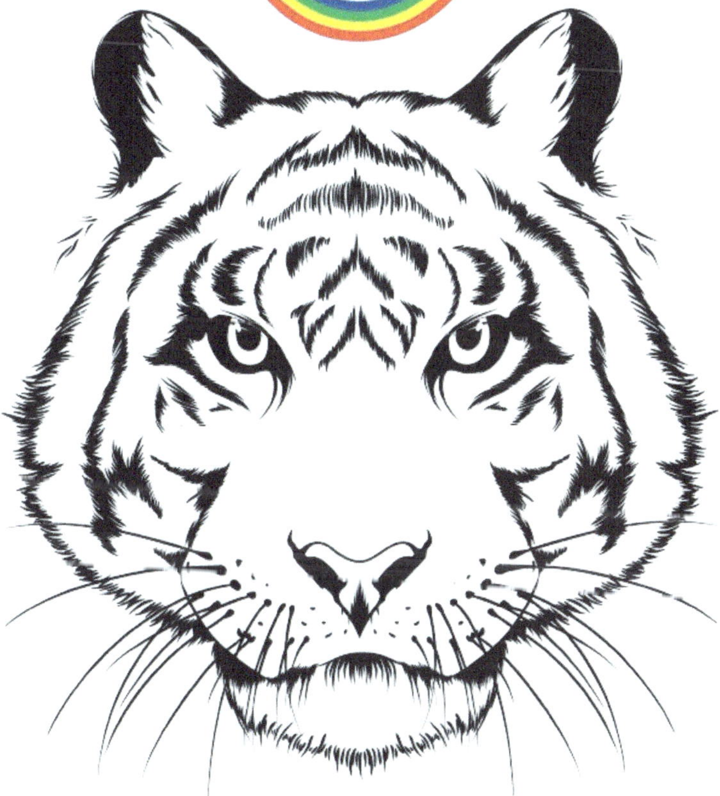

Órale!

WUNDER-PILZ.COM

CPSIA information can be obtained at www.ICGtesting.com
Printed in the USA
LVOW01s0529080414

380771LV00002B/3/P

9 780615 989839